RJ CLARK

Staycation

In memory of
Ryan ("Horse") Gholinghorst,
my brother in horror.

Your leaving was entirely too soon and, more, unfair,
but I am better for having had you as a friend.
#fuckcancer

Contents

WARNING

This book is not intended for those easily offended. If you are easily shocked and offended, please do not purchase this title.

This novel is intended for mature audiences only.

Staycation

A **staycation** (a portmanteau of "stay" and "vacation") or holistay (a portmanteau of "holiday" and "stay") is a period in which an individual or family stays home and participates in leisure activities within driving distance and does not require overnight accommodations.

Warning: The Rules

At the start, the rules of the game were simple. There were only three, which made them infinitely easy to remember. Five players and three rules, so none of them should have any problems keeping to the objective of the game. Before it began, everyone had the opportunity to ask questions regarding the rules or to seek clarification.

No questions were asked.

Again, the players were asked if they accepted the rules of the game, and each nodded in turn that they did.

And that was how it began. The game.

They called it "Staycation."

The rules:

1. Once you have your role, never break character. Ever.
2. The house is home base and a safe zone. Anywhere inside of the house is fair game, and anything outside the house is out-of-bounds. The basement, however, is the only forbidden zone and is strictly off-limits for all players.
3. Punishment for breaking any of the rules shall be both swift and severe.

Once the game begins, there is no turning back. No surrender.

The game began on a Friday—the last Friday in June—promptly at six o'clock in the evening.

And it began like this.

Day One: Fun and Games

"Honey, I'm home!" The Dad shouted in a booming but exasperated voice.

His thin baritone reverberated through the house, traveling up and down its lengths like electricity. The front door shut with a forceful and deliberate bang to announce not just his arrival, but the official start of the game. In the next room, the dining room, the good plates clattered in the china hutch, rattling what remained of The Mom's nerves. The set had been a wedding gift many moons ago from one relative or another—The Dad's mother, perhaps.

The design was loud and obnoxious, so that was a good guess. Like the dresser itself, bought thirdhand at a church flea market in Hunt's Point, the plates had seen better days. Two dinner plates had been broken, along with a dessert plate. And three Thanksgivings ago, a cup and saucer went missing. They bought a second, more expensive, set last year at the Macy's after-Christmas sale. The *real* Macy's, too—the one on 34th Street in Manhattan and not a "mall Macy's." The new set was less of an eyesore than the gifted one, and at least this Thanksgiving, everyone would have a "real" plate.

Their family loathed paper plates. And they despised plastic cutlery even more. *Silverware for the poor*, they disdainfully called it, even though they were poor. Not quite "may I have some more, sir" Oliver Twist poor, but poor enough. The family boasted that they were the only family on the block that didn't receive any form of government assistance. They didn't need "handouts," The Dad said often enough at barbecues and block parties.

And because they didn't accept any help, even though they qualified for several programs, their standard of living was well below that of their neighbors, who ate on better plates, had greener lawns, and drove better cars. He pretended not to notice, but The Mom knew he did. Other than a sizeable mortgage, they lived debt-free. Most things they needed, he bought secondhand. Sometimes, even thirdhand.

Even the family car, a 1978 gold-dusted Chevrolet station wagon, was bought used. Very used. The car set them back all of one hundred and fifty dollars and proved to be more reliable than either of them expected, even though the damned thing guzzled gasoline faster than Roger Clinton at an open bar.

But with five kids, she had to get creative to make his salary, which wasn't significant, stretch. The saving grace was the health benefits. The family paid limited out-of-pocket expenses. And they always got everything back come income tax time in April. They could complain about being unable to afford yearly vacations or summer camp for the kids, but they didn't.

The Mom had been raised simply, not in poverty. Taught to enjoy the plainer things in a life devoid of "stuff." Her family taught her to live in the present and appreciate the small, quiet moments. Whereas, with *his* family, every day was about keeping up with and outdoing the Joneses. Bigger was always better.

Appearances were everything to his parents. They somehow juggled nearly one hundred thousand dollars of debt. He was at least astute enough not to follow his parents down that path of eventual bankruptcy but could still get the kids the almost-newest tech, even if they were a generation behind everyone else at school. He even treated himself to an eighty-inch HDTV, bought used from a guy who knew a guy who got it off a truck.

They were regularly on time with their essential bills. Cable and internet could slip a month or two before they had to cough up the money. Con Edison, the power company, wasn't nearly as accommodating; they were outright thieves. A day late, and they flipped the off switch on your ass. He may not have been able to out-buy the neighbors, but he was competitive in other less expensive ways—such as claiming bragging rights for not being on welfare. It didn't cost him a dime, but he sure as fuck felt like a goddamned millionaire every time he said, "Ain't no welfare babies in my house. No, sir."

Yes, he was the resident Jeff fucking Bezos of St. Augustine Place in the Bronx.

All Quiet on St. Augustine Place

Despite his shouting, the house remained quiet.

"Unfucking real." This was not the welcome home he expected. He took a whiff of air and sighed at its blandness. No wafting aromas from the kitchen meant dinner wasn't yet prepared. *The game is definitely not off to a good start*, he thought. "I said," he began and took a long, deep inhalation of air and then released it, shouting even louder than just a moment earlier. "Honey, I'm hoooooome!"

This time, the sounds of loud shuffling feet and some sort of commotion upstairs responded. The ruckus was most likely the kids dropping like a hot potato whatever book or device had momentarily entranced them after realizing he had come home. He let go of his bag, a faded Samsonite brown leather briefcase, and it plonked to the floor, smacking it with a lifeless, dull thud.

"Daddy! You're finally home," one of the kids exclaimed. A muffled high-pitched barking rang out, and then a second later, he spied their legs through the railing, tearing down the stairs—two kids and The Dog.

He laughed to himself. It really sounded like a herd of wild elephants. He'd never noticed before, usually being a part of the herd himself.

"Daaaaaaady," The Boy said, jumping at him.

As he caught The Boy in his outstretched arms, the kid squealed. He ruffled the kid's hair and was rewarded with a small peck on the cheek. The kid leaned his head back and pointed to his own right cheek. He bent and planted a small kiss. The child snorted and shrieked simultaneously, creating a sound only possible in an excited young boy. He released the kid, and his other child, The Girl, immediately seized him around his legs.

"I missed you, Daddy," she whimpered into one of his pant legs.

He placed his hands around her head. "Well, I missed you too, baby girl. But I'm home now, and you know what?" The Girl shook her head ever so slightly. "Today is Friday. And you know what that means, don't you, baby girl?" Again, she shook her head. "It is now, officially, the weekend."

"No more work, Daddy," she said softly.

"No more work, baby girl. In fact, I'm going to be home from now on for a while because—"

The Boy squealed, and at the same time, The Dog shot off a rapid-fire succession of *arf, arf, arfs.*

"Today starts my—"

"Staycation," he and The Boy said in joyous unison.

He nodded. "That's right. I'm not going anywhere. I'm on my staycation."

"For how long, Daddy? How long is staycation?"

"Well now, I guess that depends on you, doesn't it, baby girl?"

She nodded weakly, not fully understanding the rules of the game that had only begun moments ago.

The Mom walked in, tying an oil-stained apron around her

waist as she crossed to The Dad. "Hello, love of my life," she said dryly.

"Ah, there she is." He beamed. "Miss America."

"Hardy-har-har, funny man." She smiled at him, more to emphasize her lack of anger at his remark than to acknowledge his humor. Her eyes lit up like a Roman candle in the night sky on the Fourth of July. "Oh, my god! What is that on your face?"

He winked at her, trying to act all debonair and shit. "It's my mustache. Real men have one."

"Well, I hope you didn't put it on with a permanent marker because if you did, it'll never come off. You'll die with it on your lip," she said, trying her best not to laugh in his face. "Are you hungry?"

"Of course I am, darling. I've been out all day, working hard for this family to provide a roof and security. That kind of dedication makes one hungry. Ravenous."

"You could've just said yes, you know, Bi—" She stopped herself. A horrified look overtook her face. "You... you coulda just said yes is all I meant to say."

"You sure?" he asked with a mischievous grin.

"Yes."

"Well, all right then."

"I'll... I'll go make something for dinner." She turned toward the kitchen and, in an instant, was pulled violently back to him. She wobbled into his arms, knocking The Daughter out of the way as her body pressed against his. His arms encircled her, moving slowly up and down her back. She could feel his hands moving lower and lower, toward her ass, and his hot breath on the nape of her neck. And something else. A hardness at his groin.

"Where's my kiss, Mama?"

Her heart pounded like a drum in her chest. He had caught her off guard. This wasn't something she'd anticipated, and she wondered for a second as she struggled to find her breath and words if she should have. "Your what?" she asked, her voice breaking on the *what*.

He pulled her closer to him. She could feel his heart racing in his chest, too. His breath was fast. *Excited*. Hot. Heavy. And that hardness in his pants throbbed and pressed into her lower region, her erogenous zone. "My...," he began, stopping to breathe in her scent in an exaggerated way that almost made her laugh. She would have, too, if she weren't trembling in fear. "...kiss."

The hairs on the back of her neck stood up as their eyes locked. She didn't know why she felt so uncomfortable, but she did. The way he was looking at her; lusting after her, it seemed. He'd never looked at her with such lewdness in his eyes before. It felt unnatural. And that hardness. Was it because of her? Was it *for* her? And what did he intend to do with it?

She gulped the ball of spit that had amassed in her mouth and leaned in closer to his cheek. She puckered her lips, making a duck face, and as quickly as she could, she touched her lips to his stubbly skin before withdrawing with a loud *mwah*.

"There," she said with some relief. She tried to jostle herself out of his embrace, to turn and leave, but he gripped her even tighter, coveting her. His hands seized her by her slender hips and pulled her waiflike frame back to him. She lowered her head as best she could manage and averted her eyes as The Dog continued its incessant yapping. The sound hadn't gotten under his skin yet since he was preoccupied. But it would. Soon enough. It wouldn't be long before he'd tire of The Dog entirely.

"Come on now? Seriously," he said. His breath ruffled the

hair on the top of her head. "You call *that* a kiss?"

"I do. Yes," she said into his oversized shirt.

"After a hard day's work, you think a man wants to come home to his house, his *castle*, to that? Limp is what it is." He sucked his teeth, and she noted, again, that he was not in the slightest bit limp at the moment.

The sucking sound repulsed her and made her skin crawl. He'd never made that noise before. *Who did he pick that new annoyance up from?* she wondered. If he was going to do it for the entire staycation, along with the already button-pushing eating with his mouth open, it was going to be a long, long couple of weeks. And heaven help her if it, the game, went any longer than that.

"As the man of this house, I'd say I'm entitled to more." He gripped her tighter. "Much more."

She craned her head slightly, just enough to catch sight of him leering down at her and said, "What do you—"

Before she could say the word *want*, he forced his mouth on hers. He leaned her back as her arms flailed about helplessly until they resembled, ironically enough, the lip-locked couple in that famous 1945 Time-Life photo, *V-J Day in Times Square*, also known simply as *The Kiss*. He grunted deeply into her mouth. She replied with a series of muted protesting squeals and cries.

It's going too far already, she thought as she fought against him. *This* was going too far. *But it isn't against the rules of the game,* a tiny defeatist voice in the back of her brain said. Of course, it wasn't. The game had been his idea. *He* made up the rules. Everyone else wanted to play, but she didn't. It wasn't that it didn't sound fun because it did—a little. The game itself wasn't what turned her off. It was his excitement. He was like a dog in heat about it. And now, here he was practically humping her leg as soon as the game began. She felt her stomach drop even as she continued to wriggle her body against his grip. *This was a bad idea,* she thought to herself.

For what seemed like an hour, he tried in vain to snake his tongue past her tightly sealed lips.

Too far. That is too damned far.

Eventually, he separated his mouth from hers. He kept her body bent, cradling and supporting it with his grubby hands on the small of her back and around her waist. "Now, that's what I call a fucking kiss, Mama."

Abruptly, he withdrew his hands from her body, and she dropped smack onto the floor, plopping right onto her ass. The kids peered around the doorway, their wide eyes slowly narrowing. A moment later, their footsteps darted up the stairs. The Dog stopped barking and ran to her, whimpering and sniffing frantically around her face. She saw The Dad staring down at her with a shit-eating grin on his face that said *yeah, I just did that. And you know what? I'm gonna do it again. And again. Maybe even more. And there's nothing you can do about it, is there? It's not against the rules.*

The look of horror on her face turned to laughter as The Dog's hot and repugnant breath met her nostrils. "Oohhh, Fido." She giggled, falling onto her back. "Your breath smells like butt."

"How would you know what ass smells like?" he asked under his breath.

The Dog continued inspecting her. It wiggled its rear quarter in the air enthusiastically as it sniffed up and down her body.

She rolled onto her side, laughing uncontrollably. "Fido, nooooo." The Dog sniffed on anyway. "Oh, Fido." She scratched at its tilted head, rubbing behind an ear. The Dog sighed, voicing contentment.

"Stupid fucking dog," he said as he stepped over them. "Never wanted a fucking dog." That made Fido growl ever so slightly. If he heard it, he let it slide. For now. He slowly ascended the stairs to take a shower and wash the day's hard work from his skin. But he stopped midway, long enough to call down, "Dinner better be on the table by the time I'm cleaned up, Mama. One hour, you hear?"

"Sure." She laughed as Fido ran his nose through her hair.

"I mean it."

"I know you do."

He plodded up the creaky wooden steps. A moment later, the bathroom door banged shut, and she could hear him turn on the sink faucet. She felt a momentary twinge of relief in her stomach and enjoyed the sensation for a second before bouncing to her feet. "Who's hungry?"

Fido resumed yapping.

Two Many Cooks

In the kitchen, she was quickly overwhelmed by the walk-in pantry, which had been restocked only a day or two before the game began. The miscellaneous boxes of pasta and bags of rice, the jars of red sauce, the multicolored bottles of dried spices, and the top shelf loaded with a variety of canned vegetables boggled her mind. She had no idea what to do with any of them, not to mention the assorted condiments, snacks, and carbonated beverages of the alcoholic and nonalcoholic kind.

The refrigerator had also recently been fully stocked, and she found it far easier to navigate its contents. She had her choice of a cooked rotisserie chicken, several pounds of various lunch meats, not to mention the large pizza in the freezer, along with several bags of vegetables and microwavable trays of bland white mashed potatoes. There were also several blue plastic containers of leftovers from earlier in the week, but she couldn't recall now if he'd enjoyed one more than the others.

The kids were easy enough to please. They'd happily scarf down peanut butter and jelly sandwiches with a side of chocolate milk—*oh crap, was there milk in the fridge? Yes... yes, there was*—for the next few weeks, but he would be the fussy one. He'd never really been a picky eater before, but she somehow knew that for her, he would be. Visions of him throwing a plate loaded with food at her head while shouting "You expect me to eat this shit?" raced through her head. The sick feeling returned to her stomach as she tried to guess what might make him happy tonight. He'd already proven five minutes into the game that he was full of surprises, and the last thing she wanted to do was hand him a loaded gun with the barrel pointing right at her.

She ran her clammy palms over the front of the apron, noticing the slight tremor in her hands as she did so. Frigid air spilled out of the open doors of the fridge and freezer. It swept past her face and felt wonderful against her flushed cheeks. *Everything will be all right,* she said to herself as she began pulling a myriad of items from the fridge and freezer that would make up the feast she had in mind for their first official "family" dinner. *He can't get mad if there's a lot to choose from,* she reasoned.

An hour later, the family sat down to an all-out smorgasbord of pepperoni pizza, jalapeño poppers, ham and cheese sand-wiches, mac and cheese with bacon bits and broccoli, a side salad loaded with crunchy croutons and doused in his favorite Italian dressing, a plate of French fries buried under a blanket of no-name American cheese slices that kept their form despite the time they spent baking in the oven, and some overdone chicken nuggets. The Boy liked chicken nuggets, not as much as peanut butter and jelly sandwiches, but the nuggets were a close second.

"Well, well, well," The Dad said, slithering into the seat at the head of the rectangular table. Her seat had been moved, she noticed, from the other end to the inside, opposite the kids. "You do all this, Mama?"

Her cheeks reddened again. "It was nothing."

"You're damned right it was nothing. You think throwing some shit on a pan and tossing it in the oven is on the same level as going out and working for a living," he said.

The room fell silent; only The Dog's loud exhales were audible.

He slammed a fist on the table, rattling the glasses. The silverware bounced and fell back into their respective and incorrect places. "Well? Do ya?"

She shook her head, afraid to give an incorrect response. The image of a dinner plate sailing through the air and smacking her in the temple played in her mind. The silence only aggravated him more.

Suddenly, he grabbed the table by its corners and lifted it a few inches off the ground before letting it drop. Two glasses rolled onto their sides but luckily did not shatter. "Well, do ya? Speak the fuck up. Or did the cat get your tongue?" At this, The Dog yapped a loud squelch of disagreement. He laughed. "Dog. Or did the dog get your fucking tongue?"

"No, I don't think it's the same."

"Dear," he added. She looked at him, a puzzled expression on her face. "I don't think it's the same, *dear*."

"Oh," she whispered.

"SAY IT!" he shouted, slapping the tabletop for added emphasis. The kids shuddered as though they'd been shot. They hung their heads low, and kept their eyes down, doing their best not to catch Dad's crazed gaze.

She took a deep breath and painted on a smile. "I don't think it's the same, dear." And she made certain that the "dear" sounded as sweet as apple fucking pie.

That made him happy. The tension in the room dropped back down to zero. Slowly, the kids looked up, eyeing first each other, and then moving around the table. Then, Dad said with a grin on his face, "See, was that so hard?"

"No, *dear.*"

That made him laugh. "Who knew that training you would be so fucking easy?"

The kids reached across the table, The Boy for the nuggets and The Girl for the mac and cheese.

"Excuse fucking me. Have we all forgotten something?"

The kids looked at each other and then at The Mom. She studied the prepared feast on the table. "I don't think so, *dear.* What have I forgotten?" she asked, throwing the ball into his court.

"*We* seem to have forgotten our goddamned manners." No one moved. He surveyed their blank faces one by one, slowly and deliberately, circling like a shark in the shallows. "Proper families give thanks for their bounty before eating. And we *are* a proper family, ain't we?"

She breathed a sigh of relief. *Not my fault.* The kids stared at her. "Of course. You're right, dear." She reached across the table and took hold of one of his hands and then reached to take hold of The Boy's hand as he was sitting opposite her. With a small nod, she motioned to the kids to join hands, and they did without protest, but not entirely sure what was expected of them. "How's about you lead us in a prayer of thanks, dear? What do you say?" *Ball in your court. Two for me.*

"Sure," he said, grabbing the daughter's hand in his. "Why the fuck not? Seems like I have to do everything around here."

She bowed her head. "Kids."

They observed the position of her head and copied. The Dog barked and assumed a picture-perfect downward facing dog position. Its hind wiggled in the air, making The Mom giggle.

She swallowed it before The Dad noticed and lowered her head once more.

"Lord, it's us. The Millers. We may not be what you'd call the perfect family—what with my lazy wife, ungrateful kids, and good-for-nothing dog—but you know how hard I work for this family, to provide and teach and correct where necessary. I ask for your strength and guidance in the coming weeks as we enjoy what will likely be the best staycation we've ever had." He smiled and squeezed the hands he held in his. She cocked her head and met his gaze, as did the daughter. A second later, they all smiled and laughed. "A-fucking-men."

"*A-fucking-men*," they all repeated.

"Kids." She feigned anger. "Language."

"Now, dig the fuck in," The Dad said as he skimmed a fork through the grub piled on his plate. "Jeez-us, Mary..." He stopped long enough to smirk at his wife, then continued. "And Joseph. You're no Chef Boyyy-Arrr-Deeee, are you?"

The Mom's face reddened, equally knowing and fearing that he was only just getting started. A tingle raced down her spine. The feeling of creeping dread growing in her stomach.

Kibble, And Bits, And Bites

Throughout the meal, he did that thing she couldn't stand—chewing with his mouth open. No matter how hard she tried to avoid looking directly at his face while he shoved forkful after forkful of food into it, she couldn't avoid it. It was like she was compelled to look, to see the mashed-up bits of food swirl around his open mouth and gel together into a disgusting ball until he swallowed it all in a gigantic, overdone gulp. And there was the sound. That god-awful, repulsive sound. *Schlop. Schlop. Schlop. Schlop.* The sound of the mashing, the swirling, and the chewing punctuated by bits of food escaping, often impressive distances, out of his open mouth. Her hatred of it bordered on outright misophonia, made a million times more unbearable because *he* was the one doing it.

He caught her looking at him several times, and she quickly shifted her gaze to the kids or stared down at the food on her plate. Once, she gave him a weak smile to throw him off the scent of her deep, dark thoughts. She hoped it worked. The last thing she wanted was to be hit in the head with a plate.

The Dog circled them, verbally begging for scraps. Several times, it stood nearly fully erect at the edge of the table, sniffing at the cornucopia of goodies spread out.

"Get the fuck down, dog!" He was quick to scold it, and The Dog obeyed. However, the fifth time The Dog's paws touched the table, he threw a fork at it. The utensil struck it in the forearm with little force, but The Dog made a hasty retreat, nonetheless. "Didn't you feed that fucking dog?"

It barked out an aria.

She looked at the corner where they kept Fido's food and water dishes and immediately noticed the food bowl was empty. And by the looks of it, had been licked clean hours ago, maybe even days ago.

She stood up and retrieved the empty food bowl. Fido shuffled from side to side in excited anticipation. "Who's hungry?" He barked at her. "Are *you* hungry?" He barked louder. "Who's a good boy?" He barked louder still.

"Jeezus H. Christ! Will you just feed that fucking thing already so it will shut the fuck up?!" he shouted at her. He said those last words, *shut the fuck up*, like a command more than a statement.

She rubbed behind The Dog's ear. "Yes, dear," she said as she placed the bowl on the table and began to scrape and mash bits of chicken nuggets and then mac and cheese into it.

"What the fuck are you doing?"

"I'm," she began, suddenly terrified and unsure of herself, "I'm feeding... The Dog."

"Since when does *Fido* eat chicken nuggets and mac and fucking cheese?"

The Dog yapped. She looked down at its eager, hungry face. There were bits of white foamy saliva pooling in the corners of its mouth and a thin trail of clear spit dribbling down its chin. "But—"

"No fucking buts!" he screamed, jumping out of his chair. It fell back.

The kids flinched. The Boy dropped his fork to the plate with a metallic thud while The Dog panted heavily. Its gaze remained locked on the bowl.

"Dogs," he began. He stared at her for a long moment, nostrils flaring with every exhale. Finally, he made his way into the dark pantry. He pulled on the long string that dangled from the ceiling, and a second later, the overhead light clicked on. Outside, they could hear him sifting through the shelves for something until he found it. The light clicked off, and he came back to the table proudly holding a large but half-empty bag of dry dog food. He plopped the bag onto the table and said, "Here."

"But—" she stopped herself, remembering the rules of the game.

"Dogs eat dog food."

"But, dear—"

"And our Fido *is* a dog, isn't he?"

She looked down at him. The dog yapped at her, still staring at the food bowl. "Yes, but—"

"Enough with the fucking buts. Dogs eat dog food." He slid the bag in her direction. "Now feed the fucking dog."

By then, the kids had nervously resumed eating. She looked at The Dog with concern, but it returned an almost disturbingly unfazed look. It barked so loudly that the sound startled her, and spit flew out of its mouth in all directions.

"Okay," she said finally, in all but a whisper. She emptied the crushed chicken nuggets and bits of mac and cheese onto her plate and set the bowl down on the table. *This is so wrong*, she thought. But the rules were the rules. And they all agreed to abide by them, even The Dog. She looked at The Dad, as though pleading with her eyes to make it stop—to make this stop, at least. Make an exception of sorts. But he was resolute. His face was a stone-cold *no.* Rules were rules, and there was no breaking them, *any* of them, under any circumstances.

She looked at the bag of all-natural, made from the best stuff on Earth, doggie kibble. And then to him. She stared Fido dead in the face as she grabbed the bag of canine chow and filled the bowl. When it was full, she set the bag back down on the table. A part of her hoped he would stop it now, but she knew better. And this was only the beginning. *What has he talked me into?* she now wondered regretfully.

The Dog just about went apeshit as she lowered the bowl onto the floor, placing it beside the water bowl. She noticed the water bowl was slimy with big chunks of moldy kibble floating in it. She wanted to vomit up whatever was in her stomach, just stick her head inside the garbage can and let it all out. But she knew she hadn't eaten much of the dinner she had stressed over and busted her ass to prepare. She didn't know how, but she swallowed the sick feeling down and returned to the dinner table.

The smile never faded from his triumphant face. It only widened as The Dog dove into the bowl of kibble. The crunches accentuated the silence that had fallen over the rest of the family.

Please Leave Us a Message After the—

Dinner had all but ended, even though there was still plenty of food left on the table. The eating had slowed to a crawl, and their overstuffed bellies were groaning with discomfort when the most unexpected thing happened. The family froze in their seats, trapped inside a nightmarish tableau. Even The Dog, who had devoured most of the kibble put down for him, took a breather from farting in the corner to look up in wonder and confusion.

None of them, not even The Dad, knew what to do at that moment. The Mom thought she saw the first traces of panic develop on his otherwise controlled face as the telephone on the kitchen wall, the house's only hard-wired landline, started to ring.

Then it rang again.

And again.

Still, yet again.

Its noise was unfamiliar to them. *Bbbbbrrrinnng.* No one could even recall for themselves the last time they heard that ringing sound. The phone itself was a bit of an artifact, a relic from an era before the dawn of the smartphone, when the longest cord ruled the land. It was understood, even if it wasn't specified outright, that the avocado-colored phone

22

in the kitchen was for emergencies only. Nobody worth talking to ever called on that line. Telemarketers and Russian scam artists claiming that your Social Security number was suspended and the cops were coming for you unless you paid them five hundred dollars immediately were the only ones who ever called that number. And they definitely didn't count. Even Grandma Miller used a cell phone nowadays, and the woman was ninety-four years old.

Bbbbbrrrinnng.

Bbbbbrrrinnng.

Bbbbbrrrinnng.

The ringing was incessant. Persistent.

She looked at him, then started to get to her feet when he said, "Don't."

Although she didn't want to, she remained in her seat at the table as the phone rang on and on. It was up to fifteen rings. She was counting to herself. *Sixteen. Seventeen.*

"Let it ring," he said.

Eighteen.

The phone fell silent after twenty-two rings.

She couldn't help but notice how relieved he looked as the silence enveloped them once more.

"New rule," he said as he rose to his feet and approached the telephone. "No one answers or uses that fucking telephone."

He took the receiver out of its cradle and placed it on top of the telephone's bulky body. It wasn't long before the dial tone gave way to an obnoxious beep. He returned to his seat at the head of the table. "Why don't you get me a beer, Mama?"

"Sure. Okay, dear."

She didn't give it a second thought when she reached into the fridge and grabbed a can of off-brand root beer or when

23

she popped it open and poured it into a glass. The thick layer of suds spilled over the top and shimmied down the side of the tall glass. By the time she'd returned to the table with the foaming glass, there was only static on the telephone line. A nagging feeling in her gut said that he'd probably be collecting each of their phones in the hours before retiring to bed. It was something so simple, so obvious, but he'd failed to anticipate it. As she sat back down, her mind started a mental checklist of other things he may have overlooked, things that might come in handy down the road if the game soured.

And it would.

That was about the only thing at this point she was sure of.

"What the fuck is *this*?" he said.

She turned to him and tried not to laugh as she noticed the small foam mustache on his lip. It washed away a small part of his drawn-on facial hair. The false 'stache inched down his lips in a dirty sea of foam and sweat.

"Beer. Root beer. It's what you always drink," she said defensively. "Dear."

"You're goddamned right it's root beer, you stupid bitch. Now, if I wanted a root beer, I would have asked you for a fucking root beer. What did I ask you to fetch me? Huh?"

She replied so softly she couldn't hear her own words.

"Louder."

"You asked me to fetch you a beer," she said. "Dear."

"That's right. A beer. A b-e-e-r. *Beer.*" He looked at her incredulously. "Now, why don't you go and do that."

"Sure. Sorry, dear." She rose and made her way back to the fridge. Out of the corner of her eye, she thought she saw him aiming the glass at her as though he meant to throw it at her head while her back was turned.

24

Her body stiffened, but The Boy said, "Can I have the root beer, Daddy? I like root beer."

He waited a moment, probably still considering hurling the glass at her, but then slid the drink to The Boy. "Drink the fuck up, little man."

The Boy slurped the drink, something he didn't normally do. She wondered if he did it purely for effect, as if he were saying in his own way, "I know what you were going to do to Mommy. I know, and I won't let you hurt Mommy."

The family watched in silence as he cracked open the tall red and white can of Budweiser and took his first sip. And while his expression looked as though he was about to vomit, he cheerfully said, "Ahhhh!"

The kids laughed.

"What in the hell is so funny?" he asked.

The kids looked at each other and shrugged.

He reached for the can of Budweiser, his hand moving to the exact spot he'd set it down only a second ago, but it was gone. And not just moved an inch to the right or two inches to the left. The whole thing was just gone, like it'd been sucked into the Bermuda Triangle.

"What the—" he exclaimed as he jumped out of his chair, looking high and low for the red and white can. He took a step back and was about to look under the kitchen table but stopped when he heard the kids' snickering. He looked at the kids, and soon they fell silent and grew serious. "Get me another beer," he ordered her before turning back to the kids, glaring for a long moment, then adding, "and this one better not disappear."

Words, Unspoken

After dinner, they gathered in the living room—Fido, the kids, and him. He coughed on a cigarette as she scrubbed the remnants of food off the dishes. She felt stupid for thinking he'd actually help clean up the mess they'd all made. He was adamant about his role. "Woman's work," he'd said and laughed. She could hear the volume on the television turned way up, but she couldn't make out what they were watching over the sound of the running water in the kitchen sink. *It's probably better I don't hear,* she thought. *As long as it's not a dirty movie.* She wouldn't put it past him to put on a porno while she was cleaning up their mess.

She fell onto the couch and sank into its puffy cushions. The lumpy thing had never felt as comfortable as it did just then. It was only a little past eight o'clock, but she was done. She wondered if this was how Cinderella felt in those stories—overworked and underappreciated. The kids broke out in a fit of hysterical laughter.

"What the fuck is so goddamned funny?" he said with a scowl.

They only laughed harder, and his face reddened. Finally, The Girl said, "He just said the funniest joke."

Only there had been no words spoken between them.

Satisfied for the moment, he relaxed and sat back in his chair.

The lids of her eyes fluttered and closed, the stress of the day finally overtaking her. She drifted into sleep quite easily, something of a rare feat, and there, she saw the fairy tale as it should have been or as she would certainly have rewritten it after today—herself as Cinderella, pushing the ugly stepsisters, played by the kids and him in drag, into Hansel and Gretel's oven. Fido, who at present dozed under her feet, was spared death by baking. He was a good dog, after all. But the kids hadn't asked if they could help clean up their dirty plates. It wouldn't do.

Tomorrow, she'd have a word with them in private. There was no need to get his input on this matter. She already knew what he'd say—*woman's work*, with that stupid man-sneer on his face. The kind of look that said "a woman's place is in the home or on her knees" without actually uttering the words. They rarely said the words aloud because the kinds of men that believed them were at their core afraid of women. Afraid of their power and resilience. They bore children. They nursed them. They babied their grown-ass man-babies when they got the sniffles because lord knows, they were incapable of opening a box of tissues on their own.

She knew she was stronger than him. Maybe not physically. He'd been lifting weights for the last year and a half and was starting to really bulk up. That could be a problem. A big one. But in other ways, she was stronger. The ones that ultimately mattered. If nothing else, she thought she could at least outlast him. But to do that, she'd need some rest. Her batteries needed a full-on recharge. And while it may have been a cop-out, there was a tiny part of her that hoped if she weren't in her own bed by midnight, she'd turn into a pumpkin and be done with this game—and him—entirely.

Burning for You

She was startled awake by the sensation of being on fire. It felt like her face was on fire. Her eyes flew open as she leaped to her feet. All she could hear was the sound of screaming, and it took her a second to realize the one screaming was her. Everyone stared at her. Even Fido had his sleepy eyes on her. She looked herself over and saw that she was not on fire, but there was a smoking cigarette butt on the floor beneath her. And he was grinning. Oh, how the fucker was grinning. *He threw that at me. I know he did.*

"Make sure there's dessert tomorrow night, you hear, Mama?"

She rubbed at her face with both hands, feeling for some kind of burn mark. As her index finger traced a sore spot on her left cheek, she muttered, "Yes, dear." And then she saw the tent in the front of his pants, in the area of his privates. The hardness, that awful hardness, had come back.

Gasping for Breath

Bedtime came to the Miller house on St. Augustine Place in the Bronx at ten thirty. The kids didn't put up much of a fuss about sleeping in their appropriate beds. It was all part of the game, and they understood that. He insisted on tucking them in.

She would still check on them because she didn't trust him. The kids fell asleep not long after he pulled the covers up and clicked off the overheads in their rooms. As he left their bedrooms, he slyly absconded with all of their electronic devices—smartphones, tablets, music players. Anything that could be used to make or receive a call, text, or email. Anything that could connect with the world outside of their house. They may have been young, but they were old enough to know how to use the household's gaggle of gadgets and gizmos. He wasn't about to take any chances on one of them ruining the game.

She looked at her reflection in the large mirror above the sink in the master bathroom. It looked like she'd aged a decade in just a few hours, almost as if she were aging into her role. That wasn't possible, and she knew it. She was just tired and stressed. The game sounded fun when he had suggested it. She didn't really *want* to play—they did. And it would surely pass the time until...

But now...

Now the game felt sinister, almost forbidden. Thinking about it made the sick feeling return to her stomach. Something was wrong, she decided. Very wrong. She just didn't know what it was.

Her gaze lowered, and she noticed the colorful assortment of plastic pill bottles on a shelf just below the mirror. They were "medications." She'd forgotten all about his medication. *Shit*, she thought as she picked up the inhaler branded "ciclesonide." It felt light. She shook it gently. From her best guess, there were maybe a dozen or so pumps left in it. Maybe fewer. She noticed a box of ciclesonide hiding in plain sight behind the row of bottles. In bold type, it read "Miller, Tobias." She picked up the box, shaking it violently as if to wake its sleeping contents. But it was empty. No inhaler. And next to the word *refills* was a big, fat zero.

Shit.

These Dreams

The room was dark. It felt strange and unfamiliar, the bed foreign beneath her. Uncomfortable in a way that had nothing to do with box springs or mattress covers. She knew she wouldn't get much sleep. Even though she was practically dead on her feet, she knew she *shouldn't* sleep. It might not be safe. She felt warm under the oversized comforter, clad in her thick cotton sweatpants and bootleg Adele sweatshirt from a few years ago. The singer's face, already a bad representation by a third-rate artist, had faded almost beyond recognition and was missing part of her nose. But she loved that sweatshirt. It was three sizes too big on her, but she didn't care. It was *hers*. And that's all that mattered.

He crawled into bed, slithering beside her, around eleven. His hot breath stank of beer and the cigarette he tried to smoke earlier. The smell turned her stomach. *He* turned her stomach even more. But there was nothing she could do. This was it. This was the game. And he was winning.

"Thank you for a fantastic day, Mama," he said before leaning in to kiss her gently on her cheek. His face lingered longer than it should have and then retreated slowly into the blackness surrounding them. She couldn't see his face, but she *knew* he was staring at her. He lay beside her, his legs touching hers. Slowly, he reached out to her and lowered a hand on her stomach. It felt like a sack of bricks crushing her under its weight. And at her hip, she felt that hardness pressing into her.

"You're welcome, dear," she whispered, holding back the crack in her voice.

She closed her eyes, not to sleep but to escape the waking nightmare. The night would be a long one, but tomorrow would be even longer. They would be together *all* day tomorrow. And the day after, and the one after that, and the one after that. On and on, until the game ended. And he would be beside her twenty-four seven for every one of those long, drawn-out days. At her side, and in her bed.

She resigned herself to at least rest her body, but not her mind. While her body recouped its strength for a full day of gameplay tomorrow, she set her mind to the task of ending the game without getting herself killed.

Day Three: A Cupful of Useless Shit

The second day of the game was as equally exhausting as the first. They had argued about where The Dog should sleep. He didn't want Fido sleeping in their bedroom when there was a perfectly good dog bed downstairs in the living room.

He wore her down until she eventually gave in. She was so completely drained, physically and mentally, that on Sunday morning, the third day of gameplay, she slept in later than she had planned. She forgot to set the alarm, mostly because he had taken away her smartphone, and she wasn't used to using an actual alarm clock. In fact, she wasn't entirely sure *how* to set it.

The clock was positively ancient, large with a flashing red LCD display and a ton of buttons on its body. She suspected some were inactive and just for show, like all the blinking buttons on the bridge of the Enterprise on the original *Star Trek*.

Typically, she was up by six thirty, seven on the weekends. And in bed no later than ten. She was, if nothing else, a creature of habit. Routine grounded her and kept her on track. With the game now in full swing, she had to adjust, and that took more getting used to than she had imagined. Disrupting her routine was one reason she secretly didn't even want to play the game.

But when she did finally acquiesce, it was because she thought the game would last an evening—at most. And yet, here they were preparing to start the third day.

Surely the game will end soon, she reassured herself as she stepped into the shower. A thick wall of steam quickly engulfed her, and for a moment, she felt invisible—safe, protected.

She wished she could hide in the steam until the game was finished. The demands of the game, the incessant chattering of the kids, and him—all of him, but especially his hard *thing*—felt like they were a zillion miles away. She closed her eyes, savoring the sensation of the hot water splashing against her tired body. Even without soap, she felt the near-scalding water chipping away at unseen filth. She tilted her head forward and braced herself by pressing her palms against the shower wall. *I'll just stay here until there's no more hot water,* she thought. *I'll just...*

Suddenly, she felt a cold rush of air whoosh through the room. A bumpy trail of gooseflesh appeared on her arms despite the hot water beating down on her naked body. The flimsy opaque shower curtain rattled and rippled at the unexpected gust of cold air. Its thin plastic material brushed against her skin, and her eyes flashed open wide as she sensed she was being watched.

Studied. Leered at.

She gasped loudly and spun on her heels, falling back until the fleshy cheeks of her bare ass pressed up against the cool wall. Through the wall of steam, she saw the bathroom door slowly close.

Feeding Time at the Zoo

She served the family lunch at one o'clock. They gathered around the table like pigs at a trough—a plate of peanut butter and blackberry jelly for the kids, and two boiled hot dogs wrapped in Wonder bread and some off-brand baked beans for him. She poured some kibble into the bowl for The Dog and refreshed its water, which had gotten murky with bits of food and saliva again.

It had only been two days, and already the pantry looked as though it had been raided in the middle of the night. She wondered if someone was secretly eating their way through their food stash because there should have been more food on the shelves, despite the feasts she'd made for dinner on Friday and Saturday. At this rate, there wouldn't be anything left except flour, baking soda, and other miscellaneous staples by Friday. But nothing to make a meal.

She surveyed the fridge and then the freezer. When the game began, she thought they had enough meats and veggies to last a month, perhaps even longer. Now she wasn't so sure. *Great, something else to worry about,* she thought as she waited for the water to boil.

Her stomach grumbled, but she couldn't eat anything sub- stantial. Nothing wanted to stay down. The sick, heavy feeling had returned to her belly, and she knew it was nerves. She noshed on a few potato chips and sucked down two tablespoons of crunchy peanut butter, but that was about all her stomach could handle at the moment. And even that wasn't sitting entirely well within in her bowels. She felt the mashed-up chip bits floating on a dollop of peanut butter through the river of acid in her gut. Eventually, she'd have to eat an actual meal, even if it meant forcing the food down her esophagus piece by piece.

Eating was only half the problem. She worried more about keeping it down as the game stretched on. If there was nothing left to eat, she'd have nothing to worry about. *Surely, he'll end the game if we're out of food.*

She realized, much to her own horror, that she wasn't so sure he would end the game for any reason. Not until he'd won, anyway. Or everyone else was dead.

Shitty Shoes

"Come here," he shouted. The Dog barked furiously as it tore down the stairs at lightning speed with surprising agility. He bounded down the steps after it, his face tomato-red. "Don't you fucking run away from me!"

She'd been in the pantry when the commotion began upstairs and rumbled into the kitchen, eventually spilling noisily right into the pantry.

The Dog darted between her legs, causing her to nearly fall into the shelves as it passed behind her. It panted heavily, and she noticed its eyes were bloodshot and wild with a mix of fear and fury. Fido lowered its body to the ground, not lying but preparing to attack.

She stared at the doorway with dread. The Dog growled and grumbled behind her; the sound shocked her. "Oh, Fido. What did you do?" Dread overcame her. The Dog snarled louder. "What did you do?"

"Come out here!" The Dad screamed. His shadow passed across the threshold before she saw him in the flesh. "Did you do this? Did you?"

He held up a sneaker, one of his presumably, and waved it through the air. Then the smell hit her, and instantly, she worked it all out in her head.

Oh no, she thought. *No, no, no!*

Fido had taken a shit in his sneaker. She kicked herself mentally for not anticipating this sooner. This was just the sort of thing spiteful dogs did.

"Well, did you?" he demanded.

The Dog bared its teeth in reply, as ferociously as it could muster. Its lips twisted as saliva dripped off its bare teeth. It shook its head, and gooey gobs of foamy saliva splattered against the pantry wall.

"Please, calm down, dear."

Suddenly, his attention shifted from The Dog to her.

Shit, she thought. His face was so red. Even his eyes, which were normally blue, appeared crimson. She'd never seen him this angry before. The word *fury* raced through her mind. He wasn't just angry. He was downright furious. She worried his head might actually explode. *Boom!*

A second later, without a word of warning, the shit-stuffed sneaker cracked her square in the face with a loud *slap!* Excrement went up her nostrils and splattered across her cheeks and forehead. Droplets flew into her eyes. The lonesome shoe fell to the floor like an anvil in those old *Looney Tunes* cartoons she used to watch on Saturday mornings. How she wished she could *beep, beep* and haul ass in a cloud of dust like the roadrunner now.

"Shut the fuck up," he began, stopping only to catch his breath, "you stupid bitch."

He took a step into the pantry, and she took a step back while Fido let out a deep, low growl.

She wiped at her face, angry and embarrassed. "He has to go out. We have to take him outside to go. This is our fault, dear." Her voice trailed off, and she realized she was not just crying but sobbing. The Dog whimpered in agreement. "This is our fault."

He stopped and considered her. The red slowly faded from his cheeks, along with the fire burning behind his eyes. She began to relax, but Fido did not. He remained on high alert, ready to pounce. "You're right. Mmhmm. You're right. This is our fault."

She sighed, relaxing more. "Yes. Yes, it is, dear."

"But whose job is it to take care of the house?" She held her breath, the dread coming back to her belly, knowing exactly where this new line of questioning was heading. "Whose job is it to take care of the kids? And the good-for-nothing dog?"

She felt as though a ten-thousand-watt spotlight shone on her. The Dog's shit dribbled down her face as her hands fell lamely to her sides. And while the pallor of his face had returned to normal, her cheeks now reddened behind the flecks of shit.

"Mine," she mumbled.

"What was that?"

She cleared her throat. "Mine, dear."

"That's right. And why is that?"

Son of a bitch, she thought. *Don't make me say it. Don't you dare.*

Her gaze drifted to her feet. He took another step closer. The Dog shifted with a low but menacing grumble.

"And why is that?"

"Because..." she began, but the words wouldn't come. She choked on them. Choked on the poisonous thoughts before she could vomit them out for him to hear.

"Because?"

He took another small step into the pantry, and she inched

back. Fido was now square between her legs, and her butt touched the back shelf.

"Because a woman's place," she started, crying again. The rest came through gritted teeth. "Is in the home, taking care of her family."

He grinned as she cringed at the sound of her own words reaching her ears.

"And?"

She looked up at him. "And?"

"Yes, and." He took another step, now within striking distance.

"And…" She considered his question again, and what she thought he wanted to hear; what he needed to hear to stroke his inflated machismo. "A man's home is his castle?"

"That's right. Very good. This is my castle. All of it. And every goddamned thing under this roof and on these shelves—"

He knocked several cans of string beans and creamed corn to the ground. Fido inched back, but remained alert and ready to attack. "Belongs to me. You… belong to me. Every inch of you is mine. You know that, don't you?"

"Yes, dear," she cried, nearly inaudible.

"How can I enjoy what's mine if you're not taking care of it? Why should I do my job if you're not doing yours? You know what happens if I don't do my job?"

She nodded.

"Tell me."

"You get fired."

"That's right. I get punished for not doing my job." He sneered at her. "Now, you should be punished for not doing yours? Don't you think that's fair?" She looked up at him, and

41

their eyes met. Slowly, he unbuckled the long black leather belt around his waist and slid it out of his jeans. It dangled ominously in his right hand as he grinned at her. "Don't you think you deserve to be punished?"

She shook her head and mouthed with more air than voice, "No."

"Punishment," he said as he whipped the belt above his head. "Punishment is good."

He cracked the belt like a whip and struck her in the face with it. She shrieked in pain. He whipped her again before Fido sprang from between her legs and knocked him to the ground. The belt fell from his hand as he tussled with the large dog. They rolled around the cramped pantry, their bodies blurring and blending. Fido snarled as he sank his teeth into The Dad's neck, forearm, and then shoulder. A family-sized jar of watery Italian tomato sauce shattered on the ground, hurling bits of glass and sauce in all directions. Their entwined bodies smashed into a shelf, knocking boxes of penne pasta and some canned vegetables to the floor.

She screamed until she could hear nothing but the horrible sound of her own shrill, terrified voice. Blood reddened the floor. Somehow, he flipped Fido onto his back. He bared his teeth and snapped his jaw ferociously in the air. She thought Fido looked almost rabid then. Crazed. He hovered above the snarling beast, raising a fist and striking The Dog right in the nose.

"My god! My god! Stop it," she screamed. "You're hurting him!"

He cocked his fist again, and this time, he brought it down on one of The Dog's bulging eyes. Fido howled and snapped harder at him. He punched The Dog again and again. Its hot blood painted his clenched fist red. She grabbed the belt and whipped his back as hard as she could. The bulky buckle end smacked into his soft flesh, drawing blood that made a small dot on the back of his shirt.

"Owww! Jesus fucking Christ!" He stopped punching The Dog and sat up, feeling around his back.

Fido whined and slid out from under him. Despite the fight, The Dog was only mildly injured. A few scrapes and bruises here and there. It scampered out of sight as quickly as it could, leaving a thin blood trail.

She whipped his back again, even harder this time. The dark red stain enlarged on his shirt. "Stop it! Stop it! Stop it!" *Whip. Whip. Whip.*

"You fucking dirty cunt!" he howled as he stumbled to his feet.

She whipped at his front, but missed as he swerved just enough to dodge the belt. Then he was on her. One solid, brutal slap across the face that sounded like a gunshot, and she fell back, her body sinking limply to the ground. She lay still in a heap, sobbing into a spilled bag of rice. Her face stung. The faint red outline of a distinct handprint slowly formed across the flesh of her cheek. And although she couldn't *see* it, she sure as shit felt it.

"I'll say this," he said, a grin widening on his face as he inspected the bite marks on his body. "You never broke character." He waited for her to say something smart, something cute, so he could strike her face again. When she said nothing, he added, "Now clean up this fucking mess."

He shambled out of the pantry, and she heard him cursing under his breath as he stomped up the stairs, muttering *fucking dog this and dirty cunt* just loud enough for everyone to hear.

Eventually, the bathroom door slammed shut. She imagined he would tend to his multiple wounds.

The Dog needs tending to, she thought. She'd have to find him first. *And the kids.* She'd heard the young boy screaming. Then, she wasn't sure, but she thought she heard him laughing. *Why was he laughing?*

She closed her eyes, imagining herself in a sudsy hot bath, and her body relaxed. *I'll check on the kids. In a minute...*

The thought trailed off there as she curled into a ball and cried quietly into the sleeve of her shirt.

Rabid

The Dog emerged from the fight almost unscathed. She tried not to take joy in knowing Fido had gotten the better of him, had gotten a small piece of him, but she did. Other than a minor bruise on The Dog's face, it appeared to be unharmed. It acted as if it had spent the morning playing fetch at the park and not tussling with the self-described master of the house.

Thank god, she thought.

After she'd wiped the blood—*his* blood—off Fido, she got down on the floor and rolled around, playing with the unfazed pup. Its barks once again sounded happy, and it even uttered a long trail of guttural grunts as she rubbed its belly and stroked behind its ears. She knew the sound of their joyful laughter would carry through the house and irritate him to no end, and that only made her playtime with Fido that much more enjoyable. The less time she spent with him, the better.

She thought he might end the game, but he didn't. When he finally emerged a few hours later, bandages covering the multiple bites, it was business as usual. He never mentioned the incident. Nor did he look at The Dog again for the rest of the day.

He left her alone for the afternoon, choosing to play video games in the living room with the kids. But he had that look on his face, like he was dreaming with his eyes open. Occasionally, she felt his eyes on her, studying her, examining her. *Sizing her up.* Traveling up and down the length of her body. *Stalking her.* Whenever she glanced at him out of the corner of her eye, he'd turn away. It didn't matter if she caught him red-handed or not. She knew. They both did. And whatever he was thinking, obsessing over in that head of his, she knew it wasn't good. Only, she didn't have a clue how bad it was, either.

Gots to Have Faith

Much to her relief, dinner was uneventful—at least in comparison with the earlier events of the day. Her cheek stung a bit, and there was still a red welt on the skin where he'd slapped her. But it would go away in time. "Time heals everything," her mother used to say. It was the woman's favorite expression. Her mother used it sarcastically, like when she'd missed out on getting tickets to see Shania Twain at The Garden, and endearingly in equal measure. Barely a day passed that she didn't hear the woman exclaim those words at least once. She said it to herself now, repeatedly, like it was the sacred text of an age-old spell, a panacea to end her troubles—the goddamned game. But the words somehow felt empty and weak when *she* said them.

There was an old horror movie that her dad liked to watch around Halloween. A vampire flick. In it, the fearless vampire hunter tries to ward off the evil vampire next door with a crucifix, but the vamp only laughs. "You have to have faith for this to work on me," the creature of the night taunted. And indeed, it wasn't until the hunter saw the first rays of the morning sun that he found his balls and, by extension, his faith in the religious curio, and the vamp was dust.

She wondered what it would take for her to believe everything would eventually be okay, that things would return to the way they were before the game. As though they *could* just return to whatever had once passed for normal in the Miller house. The image of their past life blurred more and more with every passing minute of gameplay.

She feared that one morning she would wake up with no recollection of who she really was and would be trapped in this life forever. She'd heard the stories, like everyone else, of actors getting lost in their roles. Believing that they *were* the characters they portrayed. That one guy, the young, handsome one who'd played that famous superhero on television, hurled himself off the roof of a psychiatric facility where he was being treated for delusions because he believed he could fly. She moved the food around on her plate with little interest and wondered if the actor finally remembered who he really was just before his body splattered onto the pavement.

No matter how hard she thought on it, she just couldn't understand how a person could just forget who they were, who they *really* were. There had to be a part, no matter how small, that tried to claw its way out, fighting to live. A lone sane voice in an asylum of lost, forgotten souls. A voice that fell on deaf ears in the end, she imagined.

She thought about that long summer month so many years behind her now, when she had grown so bored with teasing the neighborhood boys, that she pretended to be a Portugese foreign exchange student named Beatriz. Her mom caught her smoking a Tiparillo cigarette and had nearly caught her in a compromising position with their neighbor, Brad, who was playing the role of Francisco, a Portugese prince with amnesia.

Oh yes, she'd been a damned fine actress back in her heyday. But she'd never lost herself in her imaginings. *Or, had I?*

There was never a moment she wasn't fully aware that it was an act. *Wasn't there?*

But then, something else bubbled to the surface of her brain. Not a memory, exactly. Just a name—*Mary Rabinowitz.*

Who the hell is Mary Rabinowitz?

It felt like some forgotten part of her past, part of herself, was knocking on the door of her memory to be let back out. Or was it, back in?

Dead Air

She tucked the kids in that night. If he had any objections, he didn't voice them. Tucking them in wasn't her favorite motherly thing to do, but after the incident in the afternoon, she needed to make sure they were okay. And that they saw she was, too. At least, she would do her best to make them believe she was okay. She could be a damned good liar when she needed to be. After all, she almost believed herself when she said everything was still going to be all right.

"Here," she said, slipping The Girl the inhaler. "How's your breathing?"

The Girl took a quick puff from the inhaler and handed it back. "Good."

"No wheezing?"

She shook her head.

"Good. You'll let me know, though, if it starts, right?"

"Of course I will, silly." The Girl laughed.

She kissed the younger girl on the cheek. "I love you."

"Me too," The Girl said, smiling up at the maternal figure.

She slid the inhaler back into her pocket and hoped he wouldn't notice the bulge it made in her pants. For once, she prayed he'd be too busy staring at her ass to see the outline of the inhaler. "Oh, hey," she said faintly as she lowered her head to the younger girl. "Keep this our little secret, okay? Can you do that for me?"

The younger girl appeared to mull it over in her underdeveloped brain. "You mean don't tell... Daddy?"

She nodded. "That's exactly what I mean."

The younger girl sat quietly with her thoughts. For a moment, she wasn't sure if the young girl would sell her out or not. But then, finally, she whispered, "Okay, Mommy. It can be our secret."

"Good," she said before planting another set of kisses on the younger girl's cheeks.

The child swatted at her face. "Hey, enough already. I'm drowning over here."

They both laughed. "Good night, sweet prince...ess."

"Goodnight, Mommy."

She was almost at the door when the young girl spoke again. "Mommy?"

"Yeah," she replied without turning.

"What's gonna happen when I'm out?"

Her forehead wrinkled a bit. The creases appeared across her face and felt, to her, deeper than they had been only forty-eight hours previously. "What do you mean?"

"When the puffer's empty? What will we do then?"

She didn't want to think about it. "The game will be over before it runs out."

"Are you sure, Mommy?"

"Yes," she lied, hoping and praying it would be.

"But," The Girl began, then finished in a quieter tone, as if the walls themselves had ears, "what if it isn't?"

"I promise it will be," she said, just above a whisper. And she meant every word. Somehow, like the vampire killer in the

51

movie, she'd find her faith—and her courage—and end this stupid game before that damned inhaler was empty.

Silent Words

She popped into The Boy's room across the hall. He was sleeping like a rock, as he always did, and looked like an ancient mummy wrapped in a stack of fluffy blankets. She poked a hand into an opening and dug around the cave of cotton, searching for the child's head.

The tips of her fingers brushed up against the child's thick mane of curly hair. She knew it would be there, but she breathed a small sigh of relief anyway. A child physically disappearing under a mountain of blankets was just about the last thing in the world she needed to deal with. She tapped The Boy's head gently enough to register affection but not to stir the child from slumber, and silently left the bedroom a moment later.

As she headed down the hall to her bedroom, she heard the kids giggle softly in unison behind their doors.

And then she said, "Stop talking and go to sleep."

A moment later, she heard them each hop back into their beds and then their rooms were once again quiet, save for the gentle rhythm of their slowing breaths. She couldn't help but wonder if they were still silently talking in their sleep.

Jeepers, Peeper

Against her better judgment, she decided to soak her battered body in a hot bath before bed. She knew from her days of playing volleyball that neglecting soreness only deepened the pain. The stinging in her cheek would go away in a day or so, leaving only a purplish bruise to remind her of the incident. But a raw soreness remained in the small of her back from when she struck against the corner of the shelves in the pantry after he'd slapped her. It felt so tender she could barely put her finger on the area without wincing in pain. She was sure there was a colorful shade of black and blue there already. The spot was just out of view, and no matter how she stretched and bent her body, she couldn't find it in the mirror. And she wasn't curious enough yet to ask him to look at her back. That was definitely a can of worms she had zero interest in opening.

The bathroom door groaned as it pushed open, the noise audible over the running water filling the tub. Her heart leaped to her throat. She spun around ready to fight, expecting to see him grinning at her from the hallway. She imagined he wanted another peek at her body.

Instead, she saw a grinning Fido. A recently unstuffed toy squirrel hung from his mouth like a prize. He had pushed the door open with his snout as dogs often did, and she had to admit that she was both happy and relieved to see him smiling at her. She guessed they both were in good spirits despite the main event that took place in the pantry earlier.

"Hey, boy! Come here."

Fido released the toy squirrel from his mouth and obediently charged through the door and ran right into her open arms. He licked at her neck and face as though she were an ice cream cone, doing it with pure ecstasy on his face, as if this simple showing of affection was the sole purpose of his existence. The only truly selfless animal on the entire planet was a dog.

"Who's a good boy? Who's the good boy, huh?" She rubbed behind The Dog's ears, something she knew he loved. Fido shook his leg uncontrollably and sighed. "Yeah, you're the good boy, aren't you, Fido?" The Dog let out a small yap that she easily heard as *yes*. "You weren't gonna let him hurt me, were you, boy?" Again The Dog yapped. She squeezed his head between her hands and kissed him repeatedly on the top of his head. "Thank you, boy. Thank you."

After dumping a heaping amount of Epsom salt and sweet vanilla body wash into the tub, she watched as the water fizzed and bubbled. The bathwater hissed at her like she'd dumped a batch of pop rocks into a bottle of cola. She felt like a mad scientist as she sat on the edge of the tub, mesmerized by the concoction she'd created. The tub continued to fill with creamy water, and her mind drifted back to the mostly carefree days she knew before the game began.

She watched herself in her mind's eye. A week ago, maybe less, she was running through mundane tasks, talking to friends, hugging her mother. She watched herself, blissfully unaware of what was to come—the fate awaiting them. The hell he had brought down on the family. How she wished she could go back. Just for a second. Long enough to tell that younger version of herself not to play the game. It would take a fraction of a second to tell that girl, "Just say no." But it was too late. She had to find another way.

Fido nudged her thigh gently with his snout.

"Hmm," she mumbled, still more there than here.

He nudged her more persistently.

"Oh, crap," she said, jumping to her feet to turn off the water. It had almost overflowed and flooded the bathroom. The Dog sighed as if it were saying, "I know" and nuzzled down at her feet. She petted its head lovingly with a sudsy hand, then stood to undress. A layer of bubbles adorned The Dog's head like a cheap beauty pageant tiara. "Now, be a really good boy and turn around while I get in the tub."

Obediently, and without any fuss, The Dog did as it was told. She plopped herself into the tub with a loud "Ahhhh" as the hot water both soothed and scalded her tired, sore muscles. The Dog repositioned itself so it had one eye on her and the other on the door. Even though she had closed it, The Dog didn't trust what could be on the other side; what it *knew* was on the other side.

Him.

The Dog was certain that he was on the other side of the door. She knew it, too. She pictured him with an ear pressed up to the wood, desperate to hear every word, an obvious hardness steadily growing in his groin. And she felt sick.

Prestidigitation

She'd been soaking in the tub for a short while when she heard the first small knock. The Dog raised its head and aimed its attention at the closed door. It growled lowly. She expected it but was surprised the bastard bothered to knock at all. Surely he would barge in during her soak. He likely listened at the door and gauged the best time to burst through and take in as much of her flesh as possible before she threw him out. Or he would end up wrestling with The Dog again.

But he was impulsive, not stupid. Sometimes, he had the sense to think something through before acting, something about attracting more bees with honey, or some equally stupid shit like that.

She held her breath as a second knock rapped gently on the door. A third and fourth immediately followed. The Dog craned its head to gaze at her. It wore a concerned but alert look on its face. The Dog readied itself for a potential attack, priming its legs and lowering its front end closer to the ground. It looked away from her and turned its full attention on the bathroom door with its steely, intense stare.

The knocking continued. Its rhythm picked up pace, and each knock became more and more intense. Then suddenly, it stopped, and the room fell silent. The Dog released a quiet, gruff groan. She sat up cautiously in the tub. The sudsy water splashed as her body made waves in the still pool. Water spilled over the top, running over the side of the tub. She gasped as she saw the chipped gold-colored knob turn. The Dog shifted it weight. Its body sank even lower toward the ground as the beast let out a fierce growl. The knob stopped turning and froze in place.

"Hello," she called out from the tub. "Who's out there?"

"Uh." He laughed nervously, sounding as though he'd been caught with both hands in the cookie jar. "Honey, it's me."

"What do you want?"

"Uh, can I come in?"

She swallowed hard. "Why?"

"Well, it's just easier if I show you."

"Show me what?"

She heard him sigh through the door. "I don't want to ruin the surprise. Can I just come in?"

The Dog turned to her and bared its teeth. Its normally jovial face morphed into a monstrous mask of fury and aggression.

"Fido's here with me. It might not be a good idea right now," she said, quickly tacking on a "dear" at the end.

"Well, can't you just send it away? Just for a few minutes? I only wanna talk."

He sounded exasperated. There was a hard edge in his voice, and she wondered if it was brought on by the hardness between his legs.

"Come on, Ma—" He stopped just short of saying it.

The brakes in his mouth reeled back his tongue, and his jaw shut. He could have been about to say "Mama," but she knew he was about to say the other word, the one that would have ended the game right there and right then.

So close, she thought. How she wished he'd said it.

"Come on, Mama. Can I come in? Please?"

Please? That was something new. He never said "please" or "thank you." The words rolled off his tongue as awkwardly as a first-year Spanish student trying to converse with a native speaker.

She was about to tell him, "No, thank you, *dear*. Take your bullshit sentiments and shove them so far up your ass you choke on them, *dear*," when he added, "Look, I know I was out of line earlier. I'm sorry. I want to make it up to you."

He sounded sincere, and it caught her off-guard. "How?"

"Well, if you send The Dog away and let me come in, I'll show you."

She didn't want to let him in—she really didn't want to—and she didn't want him in the bathroom with her while she was both cornered and vulnerable without Fido, but she gave in. "Okay."

Her voice sounded uneven as the color drained from her face. Fido signaled his disapproval and frowned at her. She didn't know if it was the right time to explain to it that letting him in was probably safer than *not* letting him in.

He'd changed since they started playing the game. He'd become unpredictable. And volatile. He'd never so much as raised a finger to her before. But since they started playing the game, he'd become tightly wound with an extremely short fuse. She imagined him, with perfect clarity, smashing his way through the bathroom door with an ax—à la Jack Nicholson in that famous Stephen King movie from the seventies, complete with a crazy shit-eating grin plastered all over his face. For the first time, she had no idea what he was capable of. Before today, she would have laughed at even the suggestion that he'd ever raise his hand to her. In just a few short days, he'd become more or less a stranger.

The Dog scrambled to its feet and headed for the door. It tilted its head as though it was going to look back at her, but then hung its head down low and repeatedly scratched at the door instead. Her heart sank as she looked at the pitiful sight, but she knew it was for the best.

He turned the knob and tugged at the door. It resisted. The warped wood scraped loudly against the frame, eventually giving way as it creaked open. Light and a pillowy cloud of steam spilled into the hallway. He stood in the doorframe with his left arm tucked behind his back. The Dog pushed past him and rushed for the stairs, never looking back as it took the steps two by two.

"I think we're alone now," he said melodically, to the tune of the famous song by that chick who used to sing in shopping malls, Tiffany.

She turned to him, careful to keep her breasts covered by the bubbles in the bath. *He combed his hair. And what is he wearing?*

He had indeed combed his hair and had changed into his blue pinstriped suit. And as he stepped into the bathroom, the nauseating aroma of that cheap body spray he doused his entire body in surrounded her. She wanted to gag, but she knew that wasn't the reaction he was going for. So instead, she just smiled weakly at him.

"What do you have there, dear?"

"Where?" he replied playfully.

"There, behind your back."

He tucked his right arm behind his back. Then a moment later revealed his left arm and held up his hand to show it was empty, like a bad Las Vegas magician. "Nothing hiding up my sleeve."

She rolled her eyes. "In your other hand."

"Oh. This one?" He spun his arm around, careful not to spill a drop of liquid from the glass he carefully clutched in his fingers. "A tall glass of wine to help you unwind after a long day, m'lady." He attempted to bow gracefully but gave up midway through.

She reached out, and he gingerly slipped the glass into her soapy hand. The glass felt heavy. She swirled the dark red liquid around just like she'd seen her mother do on countless occasions, and then buried her nose in the glass. The faint scent of blackberry and citrus teased her nostrils. "You didn't have to do this, you know? You could have just apologized, dear." She took a long sip of the fruity wine, then wondered if he'd spiked it with Benadryl or something else to knock her out.

"Apologize for what?" he said in a serious deadpan voice.

The wine nearly shot out of her mouth. *What is he playing at?* She forced it down with one hearty gulp. "You can't be serious."

He looked at her with what appeared to be genuine confusion, as if he missed the most important part of the story and didn't get the punchline. After a moment of her intense glare, he shrugged.

"Look at my face," she said sternly, even though she wanted to get right in his face and scream. He gave no sign that he understood—or recalled. "Christ, my back is still sore, Bi—" She almost called him Billy. Quickly, she corrected her mistake. "Dear."

His eyes shone brightly. "Oh, is your back sore? Why didn't you say so, my love?" Carefully, and with surprising finesse,

61

he peeled off his sport coat and folded it in half neatly before setting it down. Her body tensed as he slunk closer to the tub. Instinctively, she sank a little lower under the water to stay just out of reach and just out of view. He knelt beside the tub and looked at her with the kindest, most loving of eyes. For just a second, she swore she had no idea who he was.

His fingers traced a line under her jaw to below her chin. He moved them up to her mouth, brushing the tip of his index finger over the soft, wrinkled skin of her lips. She flinched a little and went to say something, but he quickly pressed a long, boney finger against her lips.

When he noticed the welt on her face, his eyes softened considerably. His expression turned to one of pain, as though he felt the same sting that had caused the wound on her cheek. Careful to avoid actual contact, his fingers hovered above the bruised area of her skin. It was strange, but she actually felt the heat emanating from his fingertips. And as much as it pained her to say it, she had to admit it felt kind of nice.

He said nothing, only smiled at her as he rolled up the sleeves of his button-down shirt. His eyes remained fiercely locked on hers.

"Wait. What are you doing?" she shrieked. His hands disappeared under the sheet of bubbles and sought her delicate flesh. She quickly shimmied and weaved her body to avoid his diving fingers. "Stop it! Stop it!" she kept repeating, but his hands continued to reach for her. "Oh god, stop this!"

He locked a clawlike hand around each of her hips—

"STOP!"

—then slowly moved one down the length of a leg as the other rubbed at her lower back. Tears rolled down her cheeks, and she tried not to flinch as he pawed at her, rubbing his palm over the soreness in her back.

"There," he said, foaming at the bit. "There's the spot." As he pressed harder on the spot she banged up in the pantry, she inhaled sharply. "Daddy will make everything better." His other hand slid up and down her thigh, moving inside as it rode up toward her genitals. She squeezed her thighs together with all the might she could summon. It was enough to keep him out; for the moment, anyway. "Trust me."

Lost

Later that night, she cried silently as she lay awake in bed with his groin—and that hard thing—pressed up against her. She thought he was asleep, but after a time, maybe twenty or thirty minutes of her crying, he said flatly, "New rule. The Dog can go out twice a day."

She felt a flood of relief. He was listening to reason. He'd understood common sense.

"But no one walks that dog except me." He squeezed her tightly, pressing himself into her even more. "You hear me?"

She nodded as her heart sank to her stomach. *That's it,* she thought. The tears fell more readily now as the realization hit her with the weight of a Mack truck.

I'll never see Fido again. He's...

And although she couldn't bring the words to her thoughts, they hung heavy in her mind like dead air. *He's as good as dead.*

Day Seven: Strays

"Shhh," he said. "Nobody move. Don't even breathe."

Everyone froze where they were. The kids stood as still as statues. For them, it was just a game. They didn't know the difference between the game and reality—everything that had happened over the last seven days was part of the game—but she still did, and the look of sheer terror on his face told her he did, too.

The doorbell buzzed again. *Buzz!*

And then again. *Buzz! Buzz! Buzz!*

"They'll go away if we're quiet. Just don't make a fucking sound," he said, not sounding sold on the words himself.

But they didn't go away. The buzzer rang even more persistently. And louder, if that were possible.

She moved toward the door.

"Don't you fucking dare," he shouted in a whisper.

"It could be about The Dog. We should answer it."

"Fido! What if somebody found 'im?" The Boy said. The mere mention of the beloved pet brought tears to his eyes. The Girl cried as well.

"It's not about fucking Fido," he said resolutely.

"How do you know?" she asked.

From across the room, his head spun around to face her, and

he shot her a look. The kind that sent shivers up and down the spine and made the blood run. It was a look that said, *Keep it up, woman, and you'll be next.*

"Because... I know," he said, voice so cold it chilled the room.

Her heart sank. Tears welled in the corners of her eyes. She turned her back to him, unwilling to let him see the tears roll down her cheeks.

And that was when she knew for certain what became of their Fido; their good, good boy. Sure, she'd suspected the moment he'd come back from the walk without Fido—that had been on Wednesday, two days ago—and declared that The Dog had "gotten away." Later, at the kitchen table over dinner, he amended his original chronicle of events by saying The Dog "ran away." But he hadn't looked at her when he told and retold the story. He purposely made a point not to make eye contact with her.

But what gave him away, what confirmed he was lying, was that he didn't spoon her later that night in bed. For the first time in days, he damned near slept on the very edge, as far away from her as he could physically manage without sleeping on the floor. He was extra cuddly the next day and spoke to her in sugary sweet tones that just about gave her diabetes. And she could tell that behind the words, there wasn't a drop of actual heartfelt sentiment. Cold, empty words and half-hearted promises.

Of course, we'll find Fido. I won't stop looking until I've found him, he'd sworn to her.

But he had no intention of looking for The Dog, and he didn't even bother to pretend to.

As the doorbell buzzed on a loop, she thought she finally understood why. And it chilled her bones. He didn't need to look for Fido because he knew where he was. And he knew where he was because he'd killed him.

The harsh electronic tone of the buzzer faded. It sounded a million miles away now. She felt the sensation of leaving her body. Every part of her felt light and fuzzy, almost warm. Her cheeks flushed. The skin on her arms warmed until it was hot to the touch. The last thing she remembered thinking before her body sank to the floor was that somehow, she'd have to explain Fido's death to her parents. What would she tell them? What *could* she tell them? Dogs ran away all the time. They got hit by cars, ended up in shelters, and worse. Fido's story would be no different from countless others.

But...

They were going to be mad.

I'm dead, she thought. *They're going to kill me.*

Very mad, indeed.

"Hello," a familiar deep voice on the other side of the front door called out. A second later, a steady knock sounded on the door. "Mr. Miller? Mrs. Miller? Are you home?"

"Don't fucking answer," he said in a low voice through gritted teeth. His eyes fixed on the kids, sure they would give them away to this uninvited gentleman caller.

Knock. Knock. Knock.

"Hello?"

Knock. Knock. Knock.

"Maybe we should answer him," she offered gently.

"Are you fucking crazy? What'll we tell him?"

She shrugged lamely. "He'll just keep coming back if we don't say something. Anything."

"If we open that door, he'll never go away. He'll tell someone. Don't you see that? It'll be over." He looked at the door, then back at her. "The game will be over."

But she suspected he wasn't only talking about the game. He was talking about her, and what they had become since it began.

"Maybe that's not such a bad thing," she whispered. He shot daggers at her with his glare. "*Dear*," she added, hoping he heard the venom in her voice.

The slits of his eyes narrowed. He frowned at her so hard that she worried god might freeze his face like that, flushed cheeks and all.

"You really are special, aren't you? Say another word, and I'll glue your fucking mouth shut."

Her hands rushed to protect her lips. Joseph Beradda flashed through her head. Back in the second grade, Sister Mary Jamison had scotch-taped Beradda's entire head to shut the chatty kid up. His head looked like Boris Karloff in that mummy movie, only Joseph was encased in plastic tape and not thousand-year-old bandages. Her mind conjured Joseph, whom she hadn't thought about in quite a few years, as an act of self-preservation. She needed to be reminded that sometimes people say what they mean. After all, hadn't the decrepit old nun warned Beradda on no less than three occasions that if he didn't "zip that trap shut," she'd tape it closed? The nun not only kept her word but did one better—taped his entire head, much to the amused horror of the class. It wasn't without irony that she also recalled Sister Jamison had died from a fractured skull. Her head had been caved in by... wait for it... a falling tape dispenser.

Even without the real-world example of Joseph Beradda, the wild look in his eyes told her he meant what he said. She swallowed whatever else she wanted to say and bit down on the side of her cheek with enough force to draw blood. The sweet taste of iron flooded her tongue as she sat in silence, watching him practically shit his pants. She enjoyed the sight immensely, more than she cared to admit.

The knocking intensified. Then several long shrieks of the buzzer. "Hello? Is anyone at home? Mr. Miller? Mrs. Miller? Anyone?"

Does he know we're here? she wondered the longer he lingered at the front door. It was like he knew they were there, cowering in the dark. Someone who knew more than they should. She worried about him then. She worried a lot.

"Look, I have your mail. The box is stuffed, and it won't take anymore," the mailman said as he ceased his assault on the door. "If you don't pick up your mail, I'm going to have to leave it with the Garrigas next door."

"Great. That'll buy us enough time to finish the game," he said gleefully.

The mailman spoke again. "Look, I don't want to pry, but is everything all right?"

"What if he tells Mrs. Garriga we haven't been collecting our mail," she whispered.

He shrugged back at her. "So what if he does?"

She rolled her eyes. He could be so fucking slow sometimes. "What if Mrs. Garriga comes knocking on our door, too? Or calls someone?"

He laughed. "Who's she gonna call? Ghost—"

"I don't know," she quickly interrupted. "The cops? Maybe Grandma? I think Mrs. Garriga has her number, you know."

"Why would Mrs. Garriga call the cops?" He sounded concerned now.

She really wanted to slap him across his face. Knock some

69

sense into him. "The car is parked out front." He stared at her blankly—the elevator hadn't reached the top floor yet. "The mail is piling up." Nothing. "She'll worry. She'll think something is up. Something happened. Something bad." The light finally went off as the elevator doors opened in his thick skull with a *ding!*

The color instantly drained from his stupid face. "Oh, shit. I hadn't thought of that. If that cunt calls the cops, we're so fucking dead."

"Of course not, you fucking genius," was what she wanted to say, but instead mumbled, "I know."

"I can hear you. Are you hurt?" the mailman said through the door and waited for near an eternity for an acknowledgment before he continued. "Okay. I'll try again Monday. I sure hope you're all okay in there."

They all listened breathlessly as the sound of his heavy foot-steps tracked across the porch, then down the three wooden steps, and finally sounded farther and farther away as he walked across the pavement and away from the Miller house.

The family breathed a collective sigh of relief.

"That was close," he said, falling into the recliner, the worn springs creaking and groaning.

"He'll be back. Monday," she said in a less than relieved tone. Mr. Buchanan, their mailman for the last eight and a half years, was a man of his word. He was what they liked to refer to as a "good Christian," the type who went to mass every Sunday, confession twice a month, and liked to tell anyone who'd listen—and even those who didn't—about the power of his Lord and Savior, Jesus H. Christ. She knew now that she shouldn't make fun of Mr. Buchanan. His godliness might just save their lives.

"Nah," he said, full of bravado again. "That fruity altar boy will mind his own business if he knows what's good for him."

She crossed slowly to the kitchen. The playful squeals of the kids faded into the background. He faded into the background as well—for the moment, anyway. For now, her only concern was their dwindling supply of food. The pantry had gotten shockingly low in a very short amount of time. The fridge and freezer had grown equally abysmal looking. A thick layer of white ice had frozen over the walls of the freezer. As she peered inside at the barren landscape, she half-expected to see the good old Abominable Snowman traipse through it.

With great trepidation, she surveyed the paltry contents of the pantry. *How the heck did we eat all that food so fast?* she wondered. It just didn't seem possible. She never in her wildest dreams imagined the food would go that quickly. Did they always eat through the groceries with such voracity? She wasn't certain, although the phrase "eat us out of house and home" came to mind. If she didn't start scaling down their meals, the food would be gone by the end of next week, possibly sooner—unless the game ended first.

The realization filled her with mixed emotions. On the one hand, she'd have to tell him about their dwindling food supply. And yet, no food might prematurely end the game. He wouldn't let the family starve.

She shivered in the warm pantry. A trail of sweat rolled down her back, and the material of her plain white T-shirt clung to her moistened skin. Her hand trembled as she clicked off the overhead pantry light and wondered if he would let them starve to death.

But her mind didn't linger on the thought. The grisly image of their pale, malnourished corpses being found by Mr.

71

Buchanan weeks from now was quickly replaced by another more hopeful image—the fully stocked twenty-one-cubic-foot freezer in the basement. Salvation and salivation.

There was just one glaringly obvious problem, however. The basement was out-of-bounds and off-limits. She hadn't thought to ask about emergencies when the game began with its initial three rules, which had since expanded to four. Would he amuse himself by adding yet another new rule if she suggested ransacking the basement freezer for food?

Yes. Yes, he would. That's exactly what he'd do, she thought.

If she was going to keep them alive, she'd have to make a clandestine trip to the basement and back before he noticed. Maybe when he was asleep or distracted by the kids. She could go down and back in two minutes. Three at most. But how many times would she successfully complete Operation Food Run before he caught her? She shuddered at the consequences he'd cook up for her. She imagined one helluva spanking with the leather belt, draped bare-assed across his knees. He'd enjoy that. Looking at her bare bum. Touching it, using the belt as an extension of his own hands and fingers. And he'd enjoy inflicting pain. That was what she knew he'd enjoy the most. The pain. She thought of Fido then, and a tear rolled silently down her cheek. She hid in the darkened pantry until her eyes dried out and the redness faded from her cheeks.

When she emerged, he was but a few feet away. He grinned as she hurried past him, as though he knew what she'd been thinking, and it tickled his funny bone to no end. The low murmur of his deep, disturbed laughter followed her up the stairs.

Patience Pays Off

The sound woke her up immediately to blackness, the electronic clock by the bed flashing three fifteen. Her eyes would need a moment to adjust, but she couldn't afford to wait. The sound in her ear rang as loud as one of Jimmy Page's signature guitar solos, but in reality, it was barely above a whisper. Still, her body had shot out of bed without thinking, and she was down the hall before she even had time to comprehend what was happening. It wasn't until later, when she crawled back into bed, that she recalled the bed had been empty when the wheezing began.

She barreled through the child's bedroom door. The wheezing sounded infinitely louder now, almost desperate. Each gasp for air felt like one step closer to the grave. She clicked on the mermaid princess lamp and then swallowed a horrified gasp as the daughter's bulging, bloodshot eyes and ghostly white face stared up at her.

"Helllllllp... meeeeeee," the child gasped, pointing to her neck as though an invisible noose was choking the life out of the poor kid. "Can't... breathe."

"Hold on. Just hold on. I'm going to get the puffer," she said, darting through the door and across the hall to fetch the child's inhaler.

The door next to the bathroom creaked open, and The Boy poked his face into the hallway. "Is sister okay?"

"Yes," she said as she ran back into the child's bedroom, clutching the inhaler in her fist. "Go back to bed. Now!"

"I'm scared of the bad man," The Boy began.

Bad man, she thought, filing it away until the current calamity was dealt with. "To bed. Now!"

A second later, The Boy groaned, and the bedroom door across the hall tapped closed.

"It's all right now. Here. Here. Here," she said, sticking the mouthpiece in the girl's mouth. "Breathe." She pressed down on the puffer, and the child sucked in a gulp of mist. "Again?" The Girl nodded. "Okay." Without hesitation, she pressed firmly down on the inhaler. The child inhaled and gradually relaxed as the medication slowly expanded her airways, allowing her lungs to function normally. "Go on and breathe, kiddo."

Kiddo? Where did that one come from? She laughed to herself.

A hint of color returned to the young girl's cheeks. Her chest expanded and sank steadily and rhythmically. For now, another crisis had been averted. She wondered what would have happened had she not heard the wheezing down the hall. *I'll have to leave her door open from now on. That's all. And mine—ours—a crack*, she thought, trying to stay ahead of the next asthma attack.

She sat on the edge of the child's bed until the young girl had drifted back into a peaceful, well-earned rest. The Mom watched the sleeping child, who now looked like she was sleeping on a cloud under her princess comforter, where only moments earlier she appeared inches from death. She leaned in and kissed the child's forehead. The young girl did not stir in the slightest at the peck, but her face relaxed into the tiniest of smiles before she fell back into the safety of her dreams.

Her own comfort quickly turned to unease as she shook the inhaler at her ear. *Only a few puffs left,* she thought. The bold, black "zero" beside the word *refills* seemed to glow and pulse like a neon sign.

She'd have to somehow get another inhaler before it was too late. Suddenly, she didn't care if they ate dried lima beans for a week or not. The inhaler, getting a new one, was the only thing that mattered now. Her mind set to work on how to do it without getting herself killed. The simplest answer popped right into her head.

Killing him was the most direct way of getting a new inhaler for the child—and ending this stupid game before it went any further.

"Whatcha thinking about?" he asked smoothly.

The sound of his voice resonating in the dark hallway caused her to jump back and pull her thoughts into the present. Her heart raced in her chest. If it beat any faster, it might burst through her chest as brutally as the alien that tore out of the man's chest in that space horror movie.

"Oh, I'm sorry, baby. Did I scare you?" he said, taking a step toward her. "I didn't mean to. I would never scare you."

She swallowed. "No, I just didn't see you there. It's dark."

"I see. And how is the patient?"

"Who?" she asked with genuine confusion.

He indicated the child's bedroom with a small nod of his head. She noticed his lips ready to say something—a name, perhaps—and then quickly reformed when he caught himself. "How is she?"

"She's fine now," she said sternly.

75

Her tone sent him reeling. He hadn't expected to hear anything resembling defiance, but there it was. The first trumpet of rebellion ringing out in her chiding words.

"Where were you, *dear?*" The *dear* came out like feet on broken shards of glass, biting and caustic.

"Whaddaya mean?"

"You weren't in bed when I got up to check on the kids. Where were you?"

He took another step back. And then another. "In the bathroom."

"No, you weren't. The bathroom was empty when I got the puffer." Her words came out fast and steady, cutting him down with each new syllable.

"Well, if you must know, I was taking a shit in the *downstairs* bathroom. I thought I'd spare you the stench."

She laughed, stopping to fold her arms around her bosom.

"What? Can't a man take a shit in peace without getting the third fucking degree in his own house anymore?"

"No."

"It was that damned dinner you made. It tasted like rotten eggs. Love gone bad. Turned out my insides. Enough to make you vomit. You did this to me. Upset my stomach with your shitty cooking."

She let the insult slide. It was hardly important, given what had just happened and what was inevitably going to happen once the puffer finally ran out. "Didn't you hear... her gasping for air?"

"Nah, I was kind of passing like a lot of gas and shit. To be honest, I had a hard time breathing in there myself." He grinned at her, and it turned her stomach. "You need to be a better cook. I can handle your shitty cooking, but"—he nodded to the children's bedrooms — "it could damn near kill them."

Her face reddened as a fire sparked in the pit of her belly. *I could do it now. Just walk right up to him, reach out, and choke the life out of him while he's grinning at me,* she thought. But then, something inside her, maybe a tiny voice buried somewhere in there, the one that started the fire in her belly, said resolutely, *No. Not yet.* Her hands clenched into fists and then relaxed. She stomped past him with a huff, and her annoyance only made his grin widen and his thing harden and swell. *Fine,* she said to the voice. *I'll wait.*

Morning Routines

He didn't come right to bed. She didn't know what he was up to and didn't rightly care just then. The asthma attack left her stressed and drained. She needed to lie down and get a little rest, something she couldn't ever seem to do when he was in bed beside her. Sleep rarely came when he was there. And when it did, she had to sleep with one eye open. His eyes were always on her. It was like he never slept when he came to bed. He just spent the hours between night and morning staring at her, fantasizing about what he wanted to do to her, how he wanted to touch her. And, even worse, how he wanted her to touch him. *Where* he wanted her to touch him. *That thing in his pants. That awful thing in his pants.* She'd felt it on her back or pressing into her thigh every night since the game began. Last night, it felt harder than it had a week ago—if that were even possible. His thing felt like a piece of marble on one of those Greek or Roman statues she'd seen in her books, so hard she could just break it right off. She thought it had to be just her imagination. *It isn't possible for it to harden in degrees, is it?*

She wasn't fully awake when he came back to the room. The first rays of the morning sun shone through the closed blinds. And outside, the birds began singing the first verse of their wake-up song. There was still more shadow than light in the bedroom, and she saw him in silhouette as he crossed the room. It didn't look as though he were wearing any clothes. The stray streams of amber light reflected across his bare chest. She could almost make out the ripples of his muscles and the thick, wiry patch of hair that sprouted out of his groin.

His body felt hot as a fire poker as he slipped between the cool sheets and cozied up to her. She had her back to him and felt it press into her—hard. Harder than usual. He panted as he moved his hips and rubbed his awful thing across her clothed buttocks. His breath stank, not just of neglect but of cheap beer and cigarettes.

So that's what he's been doing all night...

He wrapped an arm around her and rubbed her stomach, then inched higher toward her chest. She gasped softly as he grabbed her left breast and began to squeeze and knead it through the thin material of her nightshirt.

"What... what are you doing?" she cried, trying her best to roll away from him, but he threw his other arm around her waist and held her firmly in place while he continued to feel up her breast. "Stop it. Let me go."

"You know, darling wife o' mine, I feel you owe me a little something after getting me all sick with your shitty cooking. And I want to collect it. Right fucking now."

"What... what do you want?"

But somehow, she knew. She just knew. He didn't have to say it, and he wouldn't. Instead, he took hold of her hand and guided it to the hard thing between his legs, closing his hand around hers so that her hand now made a tight fist around his throbbing thing. She felt his hot, stinky breath brush over her face, and she fought the urge to retch. Slowly, he began to pump her fist up and down the length of his hardness. His breathing quickened. She could feel his heart pounding in his chest as her hand went up and down his thing.

"Faster." He groaned. "Do it faster." She gripped him tighter and then pumped it faster. He moaned loudly into her ear. Suddenly, he gripped her hand as though telling her to stop, then guided her hand away from his hardness and to his mouth. She heard a horrid *ptooey*, and a second later felt his saliva coating her palm. He panted rigorously and moved her hand back to the thing between his legs and motioned for her to continue. His legs shook uncontrollably as her greased-up hand touched his engorged, tender flesh. "Faster. Harder," he groaned, and she did as she was told. All the while, she had her hand wrapped around his awful thing, his hand squeezed at her breast. "I'm nearly there."

"Where," she whispered.

"Don't stop. Keep... going." He removed his hand from her covered breast and slid it down her stomach and then up her shirt. His fingers traveled the length of her torso until it clamped down hard on her bare breast.

"Ahh!" she groaned as his fingers squeezed at her breast and flicked over her nipple until it was as hard as the thing between his legs. It was wrong, what she was allowing him to do to her. She knew it. She didn't need the voice to tell her that. But, at the same time, the sensation that shot through her body from his touch on her breast was electric. She couldn't describe it if she tried. And while she didn't want him to continue, she didn't want him to stop, either.

"Shit," was all he said as thick globs of hot liquid erupted from the hardness and dribbled down her fingers. She couldn't believe how it felt on her skin. Slimy. Sticky. Hot to the touch. His fingers pinched at her nipple as though they were tiny teeth trying to suckle at her breast. Every part of him seemed to writhe and shake on the bed as shot after shot of liquid came out of his hardness. He bit down gently on her shoulder as the final spurt came, his legs fluttering like a piece of paper helplessly caught in the wind.

After a moment, his breathing slowed, and the hardness receded, shrinking back into itself. He removed her soiled hand from his thing, but kept a firm grip on her bare breast. She held her hand up, unsure what to do next, and saw the globs of white goop in the growing light of morning. She patted at a glob with her finger. It was cooler now. She wanted to laugh because the stuff kind of felt like a booger, and she wondered if it would harden on her skin in a mosaic the way snot would.

He rolled her onto her side and came up behind her. The thing between his legs, no longer hard, touched her bum limply. She felt him place a light kiss on her neck as his hand squeezed around her boob. As she wiped the fluid onto the front of her shirt, he twitched against her, and she knew he had fallen asleep.

Finally, he was sleeping.

I could do it now. He'd have it coming, too.

She waited, and after a short time, the voice finally said once more in a strong, unwavering tone—*no, not yet.*

Unsolved Mysteries

It was gone. That was all she knew. Not how or when, just that it was gone.

The car.

Their driveway was now empty, a sole dark oil stain on the concrete, the only sign that a car once stood there. *Their* car once stood there. Her first thought as she peered through the blinds in the bathroom was that the car had been stolen overnight. Theirs wouldn't have been the first or the last car boosted overnight in the neighborhood. She remembered just a few weeks back the Abdallahs had their car lifted from right in front of their home in broad daylight. Gossip around St. Augustine Place was that the theft of the Abdallah family's 2012 Ford Explorer had been motivated by anti-Muslim sentiment. She couldn't believe it—wouldn't believe it.

The Abdallahs were the nicest family in the development, outside of the Millers, naturally. They were an honest, hard-working family that looked out for their neighbors. The Abdallahs were friends to all, chasing the elusive dream that brought them to this country. There were seven of them, just like the Millers, with an eighth Abdallah on the way in December. Maybe that was one reason she liked them so much; the Abdallahs reminded her of the Millers. And now, they'd both had their vehicles stolen right out from under their noses.

Who the heck would want a very used 1978 gold-dusted Chevrolet station wagon when there's a fairly new Escalade two doors down? And that was when it hit her—*no one.* Absolutely no one would want their crappy car. It wasn't worth anything, not even for scrap. The thing had an eight-track player for Christ's sake. An eight-track player! They only had the one tape—*John Denver's Greatest Hits*—and it was on its last legs. She doubted there was a gang of car thieves scouring St. Augustine Place for a barely running jalopy decked out with a vintage eight-track player. No, not likely at all.

And then it all made sense.

Of course.

How could she have been so stupid not to have seen it sooner?

He hadn't been *relieving* himself downstairs when the young girl suffered her asthma attack.

He hadn't even been *in* the house when it happened.

He was outside moving the car. He had to move it because Mr. Buchanan, their mailman, left him no other choice after mentioning the car in the driveway. If the car was still sitting there on Monday, he'd ring the bell again or go next door to the Garrigas just as he'd said. Or, worse, bring the police to do a welfare check or break down the door. A week ago, she'd have been scared to have the cops at their door, but now? Now, she'd throw open the door herself and show them in. He'd made up that silly lie about her food making his tummy upset. And then made her touch it, that thing between his legs. He lied about *everything.* She suspected he just wanted her to touch him there all along.

Wait! He left the house, she thought excitedly. *He broke the rules! He has to forfeit the game.*

83

She turned on the shower and stepped into the tub, pulling the curtain behind her. The steady stream of hot water relaxed her stressed-out muscles. And the more she thought about the game and about him leaving the house, the more she allowed herself to relax.

It's over, she thought with a smile. *It's finally over. And he lost.*

But, the nagging voice returned once more to have the last word.

Don't be so sure.

A Happy Tune

"What the hell are you doing?" he asked.

"What do you mean?" She hadn't been doing anything as she walked into the kitchen. Maybe she was running a hand through her wet hair, but she didn't know why that would agitate him.

"That sound. Why are you making that sound?"

She was about to ask what sound when she caught herself about to do it again. Whistle. She'd been whistling one up-tempo song or another since her revelation about the game in the shower and continued to do it unknowingly as she bounced into the kitchen to make the family breakfast. "Oh, I don't know, dear. Just... happy, I guess. Can't a girl be happy anymore?"

"What the fuck do you have to be happy about this morning?" He practically grunted at her.

She shrugged. "Stuff." The smile formed on her face without her even being aware of it. *Checkmate. I got you in checkmate. Game. Fucking. Over.*

"What kinda... *stuff?*"

She poured herself a small cup of coffee, something she rarely drank but found she needed to drink to get through the day since the game began. That was one thing she would be happy to see end with the game. The instant coffee tasted like rotten water—if such a thing existed. The caffeine buzz always wore off after a couple of hours, and she had to keep guzzling down more of the stuff if she wanted to stay awake.

She was about to answer him, the words on the tip of her tongue—

—*you broke the rules. The game is over. I've picked out your punishment*—

when she saw it.

The large handwritten sign hanging on the door of the refrigerator:

The New Official Rules of the Game

1. *Play your part at all times.*
2. *Home is safe. Basement is out-of-bounds.*
3. *Punishment is severe for breaking any of the rules.*

And then, under the three basic rules they had all agreed upon eight days ago when this folly first began, was this:

1. *Daddy is the only one allowed to leave the Miller house without question or notice if it's for the good of the whole family.*

She nearly spat out the brown water in her mouth as she read the revised rules. "When... when did you do that?"

"Yesterday," he said with a grin, lighting a cigarette. He took a long drag without a single cough, and then, accented by puffs of smoke, added, "Just after that foul supper you fed me. The one that made me sick last night."

He didn't say it, but she knew what he was thinking. It was written all over his smug face: *Check, you stupid cunt. Your move.*

Caught Between Two Bad Choices

Dinner that second Saturday night consisted of grilled cheese sandwiches, though to be honest, it was more grilled bread than cheese. One measly slice of an orange cheese-like substance, which seemed to be unmeltable no matter how long it was pressed to the heat, cushioned between two slices of nearly stale white bread. The meal was rounded out with a handful of chips that had also gone stale, thanks to someone forgetting to close the bag after they helped themselves between meals. There was no milk left for the kids, so she mixed up some purple powder in a glass of water, and they seemed content to wash down the paltry meal with the resulting sugary beverage.

God forbid they just drink water, she thought as she stirred the powder, mesmerized as the water turned a blood-red color. *Even I can turn water into wine. Hardly a miracle.* She didn't know why she thought that. It wasn't like her, not that she was convent-bound or anything, but she held onto a certain amount of reserve for the Lord Almighty. Maybe it was fear coupled with a few drops of reverence, but she didn't like to taunt Him and didn't take kindly when others did, either. Guilt by proximity, she called it. Truthfully, she'd rather not get struck by a stray bolt of lightning raining down from the heavens if she didn't have to.

He eyed the meal with discontent but said nothing, washing down the sticky sandwich bites with mouthfuls of beer. Their food supply was running low, but his supply of beer always seemed to replenish overnight. If he had 'a coupla beers' before bed, there'd be two empties beside the sink and two fresh cans of Bud chilling in the fridge in the morning. She didn't notice it—the Miracle of the Beers—at first. And she wasn't entirely sure when she finally caught on that the beer flowed endlessly in the Miller household. Thursday night, maybe? Friday? It didn't matter. She knew how he was doing it. His skills of prestidigitation weren't all that impressive. He was no Doug Henning. Hell, he wasn't even on par with that goth guy who'd been relegated to doing Vegas shows after his act never matured beyond black eyeliner and pitch-black hair dye.

Aside from a fresh supply of food, there were cases of beer in the basement. She knew this. She'd seen the stockpile of red and white cans with her own eyes just days before the game began and the basement became out-of-bounds. He'd been going down to the basement to fetch more beer. He'd broken the rules again, but she couldn't say anything. She was too afraid to. What if he locked the door? Or worse, nailed it shut? He could do without the liquor, but they couldn't live without the food. And with his unpredictable moods, she wouldn't put it past him to do something dramatic to ensure no one could enter the basement ever again.

How she'd love to call him on it. Empty all the beers in the fridge. Pour them right down the sink and then see what he did. Ask him to explain how they just magically reappeared overnight. *It was a miracle. A fucking miracle,* she could hear him say now. Knowing something isn't the same as being able to prove it. She'd have to catch him coming out of the basement if

89

she wanted to end the game. And, more importantly, be careful herself when she ventured down there to forage for more food.

She swallowed a large mouthful of dry, overcooked bread and winced. As she gulped water to wash it down, she wondered what end she'd ultimately prefer. Death by starvation or death by her husband if she tried to end the game. The former seemed less painful to her now.

The Bad Man

She decided Sunday was the day to venture into the forbidden basement. There was no other choice, really. What food remained would be gone come Monday night. Perhaps even sooner. The Mystery of the Disappearing Food was a case she'd yet to crack, but she could get on with that later—after she'd replenished some supplies.

"Mommy, I don't want to," The Boy said with a frown. His little face scrunched up and was on the verge of waterworks.

"Why not? I thought you loved playing with your daddy?"

"I did," The Boy cried, the first tears rolling down his cheek.

"Well then, why won't you play with your dad tomorrow? I need you to play with him after breakfast. It's really important you do this. Do you understand? Real important. But you have to do it upstairs, okay? Here, in your room. Can you do that for me? Can you do that for... Mommy?"

The Boy seemed to ponder the possibility, and then really let loose with the tears. His face turned bright red, and he wailed. "No, Mommy. Please don't make me. Please."

He was testing her patience. She wanted him to understand but couldn't tell him and have him ruin the plan entirely. "I don't understand, baby. What's wrong with—"

And then she remembered what The Boy had said just one

night ago as she ran into the bathroom to fetch the puffer. She'd almost forgotten about it. No, she *had* forgotten about it. She had chalked it up to either an overactive imagination or the remnants of a vivid dream. But now, she wasn't so sure it was either. This game had twisted into a waking nightmare, hadn't it? If it *had* ever been fun, the game stopped being fun for her days ago, and her mind was now occupied almost exclusively with thoughts of how to end the horror once and for all.

The Boy had said it, and she didn't listen. She forgot. Moved onto other things. But now, it was all she could think of. There was nothing else.

I'm scared of the bad man, The Boy had said.

And there was only one man in the house. One very, very bad man.

Before she could lasso the thought, it formed in her head.

I am, too.

The First Interlude

Grandma "Cast-Iron Cassandra" Miller lived over twenty-five hundred miles away from St. Augustine Place in fabulous Las Vegas, Nevada. Cassie Miller had never been sick a day in her life, not so much as a sniffle. Even as a child growing up in Greenpoint, Brooklyn, she earned her perfect attendance certificate every year at St. Anthony's Catholic School.

There had been a severe strain of the flu virus in Greenpoint back in the brutal winter of 1933, and the mumps and the pox made their appearance the following year. Five of her classmates died in 1934. The fatalities numbered higher in the upper classes. At one point, Cassie heard that two dozen kids died during those two years, possibly more.

But Cast-Iron Cassie developed neither a mump nor a pox and sneezed but once during what would later be called the "winter of blood" throughout New York City. Cassie was stronger than most of the kids her age, and she knew it. Even St. Anthony's resident bully, Gary Graves, would duck into a corridor or stairwell if he spotted Cast-Iron Cassie coming his way.

She was the youngest of eight siblings, five girls and three boys, and she'd outlived them all. Two of the boys, Stephen and Joseph, died in a house fire in '27. Someone had been playing with matches in the cellar of a neighboring house when it caught fire, and the boys and their friends couldn't escape the flame-engulfed brownstone. She barely remembered either of them. The war took her brother John, her favorite, in '42. Her eldest sister, Eunice, fell overboard from a sailboat off the Long Island Sound and drowned over Memorial Day weekend in '47. Cancer took both of the twins a year apart—Melanie in '53 and Melodie in '54. And Janet hanged herself in her bedroom closet on June 7 in 1968, the day after Bobby was assassinated at the Ambassador Hotel in Los Angeles. Her parents passed in the fifties, both reaching well into their seventies.

Cast-Iron Cassie was the last of the original Greenpoint Millers left standing.

She'd married a respectable fellow by the name of Maurice Miller when she was forty, late for her generation, but she always joked that she'd just been waiting for the right fella to come along, and Maurice sure took his sweet-ass time. They'd had four children, the last one, her only son—William "Billy" Miller—born when she was fifty-one years old.

The Millers were strongly cautioned to cease bearing any more children after their second, but they were Catholic and did what Catholics did best—make more Catholics. It'd been what doctors referred to as a "difficult" birth. The umbilical cord nearly strangled baby Billy to death before the infant even gasped its first breath. When he finally made his first appearance, after quite a bit of adjusting, he wasn't breathing. Everyone in the room, including Cast-Iron Cassie, feared the boy was dead on arrival, but to everyone's surprise, baby Billy soon gasped and screamed at the top of his lungs for forty-seven minutes straight. If anyone in the Miller clan had inherited Cassie's unsinkability, it was Billy. Perhaps that was why her son was her unofficial favorite child—because no mother has an "official" favorite.

She lost Maurice when Billy was still quite young, and he became the only man in her life. A heated word rarely passed between them, if ever, and he took unusual pride in the phrase "mama's boy." Several of his girlfriends had dumped him because they'd grown tired of living in Cast-Iron Cassie's shadow. But not Denise. She was as strong-willed as Cassie had been in her youth and had no problem telling the matriarch "no" when her husband wimped out at the sight of mommy dearest.

Despite her misgivings, Cassie approved of the marriage and welcomed her new daughter-in-law into the family. She wouldn't live forever, no matter how it seemed, and Denise was the perfect stand-in to take care of her darling boy once she returned to dust herself. But she'd never tell Denise that. It was far more entertaining to go on letting her daughter-in-law believe that she hated her than to admit that her son had chosen a newer model of his own mother to marry and with whom he could eventually procreate.

It was that connection, the ever-present phantom umbilical cord, that told Cast-Iron Cassie something was wrong. She didn't know *what* exactly, but something just *felt* off with the Millers on St. Augustine Place. Billy was on vacation for a week. She knew that. Still, it was not like him to go more than a day without checking in with his mama. And now it had been over a week, close to ten days. What really nagged her insides was that she couldn't get him on the phone. His cell phone went straight to voicemail, and the home phone rang busy for a brief time and then also went to voicemail.

The digital mailbox attendant cut her off last night when she tried to leave a message, another message—her fourth. *I'm sorry, but the message you're trying to leave cannot be delivered at this time. System full. Please try again later. Goodbye.*

Cassie thought the "goodbye" sounded too pleasant, almost joyful, like, *Haha, you can't leave a message. Ha. Ha. Ha. Ha. Haaaaa. Haaaaaaaaaaa.* It annoyed her, made her want to reach through the copper wires and strangle the taunting robot on the other end. But she knew her agitation wasn't so much with the telephone attendant as it was with her negligent son. When he finally did reappear, she planned on giving him several pieces of her mind.

That was assuming he *did* materialize.

Well, that's just stupid talk now, Cassie. Why wouldn't Billy come back from vacation? she thought as she slipped a crisp, new twenty-dollar bill into the slot machine.

Cassie, the voice in her head said.

Yes, Cast-Iron Cassie replied.

Why wouldn't Billy come back from vacation?

Cassie pulled the lever, and the tiles on the screen jumbled and danced in a blaze of flashing lights and computerized music. She stared at the screen waiting for the tiles to fall into position and spell out the answer.

Cassie?

Huh?

Why wouldn't he come back from vacation?

The first tile locked into position with a clang. A cherry.

Because...

Then the second tile froze. Another cherry.

The tiles in the last row flipped frantically.

Because...

Yes?

Because... he can't. Because something happened to him. That's it, isn't it? Something is wrong? Something is terribly wrong. Isn't it?

The tiles stilled. On the screen, three cartoon cherries stood side by side on the pay line. Her eyes saw but didn't see. Cassie felt chilled, ice cold. And then, suddenly, a red alarm howled and flashed, wailing as the machine vomited coins out of its dispenser.

All told, the machine reluctantly gave up five grand in shiny gold tokens, but by the time it stopped spilling its riches, Cassie was crossing the Circus Circus parking lot to her Lexus, talking to her travel agent about booking a flight to the East Coast. Her boy needed her. She was sure now that her boy was in trouble. Big trouble. But she'd be there soon enough to rescue him.

The thought that Billy Miller was already dead never occurred to her.

Day Twelve: Dead on Arrival

"Rowww, rowww, rowww your boat! Gently down the streeeeam," the kids screeched in unison. The Wi-Fi had gone out late last night and still hadn't come back on, so the kids had taken to singing silly songs to amuse themselves.

But he was not amused.

The sound of their squeaky voices singing another round grated on his last nerve. His right eye had twitched twenty minutes ago, right about the same time he cracked open his second Bud of the morning.

She noticed he was drinking more now. One or two beers at night with dinner had turned into four or five throughout the day and then two or three with and after dinner. At least the liquor made him sleep soundly in a drunken stupor. The thing between his legs stirred less the more he drank. Something else she was grateful for, and she'd hold on to every silver lining she could find.

"Row, row, row your boat. Gently down the stream! Merrily, merrily, merrily. Life is but a dream."

Tap. Tap. Tap.

It was hard to hear at first. A weird metallic sort of sound, like metal scraping on metal. She thought the sound was just her imagination. While she was in the kitchen, it sounded far away. Outside, even. But as she walked through the kitchen into the living room, the sound grew louder. Not so loud that it was obvious, but she heard it.

Tap. Tap. Tap.

The kids giggled before taking a deep breath and launching into a rousingly off-pitch rendition of "London Bridge," complete with bad British accents. And in those few seconds of quiet, as they sucked in as much air as their bodies could hold, she stood perfectly still in the middle of the living room and heard the noise clear as a bell.

Tap. Tap. Tap.

The noise was coming from below her feet, deep in the bowels of the Miller house—the basement, which was still very much out-of-bounds.

"London Bridge is..."

She wanted to go downstairs and see what it was. It could be a leaky pipe or gas leak, and then he'd have to end the game. *Right?*

"... falling down, falling down..."

Right?

"London Bridge..."

No, the voice told her. *He'll never end the game.*

She didn't know why, but her heart raced. *Then let me do it now. I could just go in there and hit him over the head with—*

No. Not yet.

As a kid, she'd been petrified of the basement. She'd stayed up late at a girlfriend's house watching *The People Under the Stairs* and came home convinced a horde of zombified homeless people lurked in their cellar, and it was years before she realized how silly it was to think that. She reckoned there had to be better places for a hungry crowd of zombies to stake out, like

Mar-a-Lago.

Eventually, like all the things we fear from our childhood, her fear of the basement faded into an amusing memory. Now it took everything she had not to tear open the basement door and run down the wooden steps. But, like bashing in his head, it would have to wait. By the time the kids warbled "Itsy Bitsy Spider," the noises in the basement had stopped. Her heart, however, still pounded away in her chest.

"… up the waterspout. Down came the rain and—"

"Jesus H. Fucking Christ." He moaned as cigarette smoke billowed around his head. "You is giving me a fucking headache. The headache to end all headaches. Now give it a rest, won't you?" The kids understood it wasn't a request. It had been a command.

The Boy looked at him defiantly. "Washed the spider out."

He slammed a fist on the table. It sounded loud as a gunshot and made everyone jump. She ran back into the kitchen as another sound came up from the pit of the basement, a faint, pained moan.

"Out came the sun."

"I'm only gonna say this one fucking time, you hear me, boy?"

The Boy was defiant. "And dried up all the rain."

"You cut that singing out now."

She stood in the doorway, nervously fidgeting with her hands. The Girl looked at her, begging her to help. Pleading with her eyes to make him stop before something bad happened. *I'm scared of the bad man. The bad man. The bad…*

"Come on now, dear. Why don't you come into the living room and watch some television? Let him be."

"Everything is out. The goddamned cable. The internet.

What am I supposed to watch? Huh? Goddamned Mister Fucking Rogers?" He threw the chair out from under his ass and rose to his feet. "Don't you dare tell me what to do, woman. You stupid cunt. This is my house. I make the rules. Me. Me! I'm the fucking king."

"I know, but—"

"I know, but," he said, mimicking her in a voice that made her sound mentally challenged. "Say 'I know, *sir*.'"

"What?"

"But the itsy bitsy spider..."

"Say it, woman. 'I know, sir.'"

"... crawled up the spout again."

"No," she said with resolve in her voice that even took her by surprise.

"The itsy bitsy—"

"Ahhhhhh," he screamed as he lunged at The Boy, seizing him by the throat. "Now, what did I tell you? Huh? What the fuck did I tell you?"

"Let him go!" She eyed the coffeepot on the counter. *Now.*

She could do it now. Her hands shook furiously as she moved toward the potentially lethal vessel. In her mind's eye, she saw herself pick up the coffeepot, which was three-quarters full of hot liquid, and smash it into the back of his head. Not just once, but repeatedly. Even after he crumbled to the ground and his body seized, she brought the pot down onto his head with all of her might until his skull split open like a watermelon and skull bits and brain matter spilled onto the floor.

But the voice was resolute. *Not yet.*

The Boy struggled to breathe. It was amazing how quickly his pallor changed to a bluish-purple as he gasped desperately for air. He tightened his grip around the boy's throat. She'd never seen him like this. Never. Something had snapped in his head, and there was a distant, far-off look in his eyes. The lights appeared to be on, but nobody was home upstairs. He looked crazed. Mad.

He *was* crazed. Like a rabid dog with big red eyes and foam dripping out of its mouth. The Boy's legs thrashed in the air as his hands pecked at the fingers wrapped around his throat, choking the life out of him.

She saw the light dimming behind The Boy's eyes, and she screamed like a banshee in a voice so high, so shrill that the glasses on the table rattled and shook, threatening to shatter and send hundreds of tiny shards of glass hurling through the kitchen.

"Stoooooppp iiiiiiiiiiiiiiiiiit!"

He let go of The Boy's throat and covered his ears as she continued to scream. The Boy fell against the counter and then slumped to the floor, gasping for air, two large bruises forming on his neck. The color in his face lightened but remained blue as he sucked in as much air as he could comfortably manage. She hurried to comfort the shell-shocked child and kept her body firmly between father and son.

She wanted to do it. She wanted to do it so badly, but the voice whispered, *No.*

He stepped toward them, his long shadow painting them in black. "How old are you supposed to be?" he barked at the gasping child.

"Not now, dear. Please."

"I wasn't talking to you," he said, taking another step closer. The Boy cowered into her chest, and her arms instinctively shielded the child's head like a helmet. "You best answer me when I ask you a question... *boyyyy.*"

"Can't this wait? You damned near—"

The young girl was crying now. She wiped at her wet eyes with both hands as a steady supply of tears spilled down her face.

"You damned near killed him. Leave him alone. Leave us alone."

Before she could move, or even think, he pulled a knife out of the block on the counter, the largest, sharpest knife in the set—the butcher's knife. As he pointed it in their direction, a menacing grin overtook his face. The blade shimmered as it caught the light. He tossed the knife from his left hand to his right, taking immense pleasure in the terror the movement created. The young girl howled even louder. Slowly, he approached the cowering bodies on the floor, the glimmering, pointy tip of the knife leading the way.

"Oh, dear god. Help me," she murmured.

The young girl screamed and howled as her face reddened and grew slick with a watery trail of nonstop tears.

He stopped and smiled. "This," he said, holding up the knife as though it were a prop on display, "is god." Then he laughed and laughed, sounding just like Freddy Krueger from those old *Elm Street* horror flicks. "Now, I'll ask you one more time, *boy,* and if you don't answer me, I'ma slice your ma's throat like it were a *tamatah.*"

She saw that awful thing between his legs twitch in his pants.

The young girl screamed even louder.

The commotion was so loud she was sure the neighbors could hear the screaming and the crying. She wouldn't be surprised if Mrs. Garriga had her ear pressed up to their front door while calling 9-1-1 on her cell phone. *Good. Let them come. Maybe they'll shoot the bastard, and I'll win. Game over.*

But nobody came, and nobody would come. She was on her own.

"How old are you supposed to be, boy?"

The young boy shrank further into her chest. She hugged him tightly, pulling his body as close to hers as she could manage. The child let out a long, almost agonized sigh and then turned his head toward him and the sharp end of the fourteen-inch stainless steel kitchen knife. Slowly, and with unusual grace and precision, the child stood as though his body were uncrumpling itself bone by bone, tendon by tendon, and muscle by muscle. When he finally stood fully erect, The Boy appeared calm and showed him absolutely no fear.

"How old?"

The Boy looked at his sibling, confused, and then returned his gaze to the man holding the knife. "Eleven," the Boy said unconvincingly.

"I see. Eleven fucking years old." He lowered the knife and bent down to the still sobbing young girl. "Is he eleven fucking years old, darling?"

She tried to speak, but only dead air came out of her mouth. In the end, all she could do was nod until her head damned near popped off.

"Eleven years old and still singing baby songs. Are you a fucking baby, *boy*?"

"No."

"You can call me sir from now on, too, I think." The Boy stared at him blankly. "Say it. Or so help me..."

"No, sir."

He smiled and tossed the knife into the sink. It landed with a clang, followed by the sound of breaking glass. Lackadaisically, he took a beer out of the fridge and headed for the living room.

"I don't know what the fuck is wrong with this family."

When he was gone, The Boy fell backward like a tree in the forest and landed right in her open arms.

Endless Days

The hours of the day seemed longer without the wonders of the internet to keep the family entertained and distracted. He fell asleep on the love seat and hadn't so much as farted in his sleep since one o'clock. It was now half-past three. The kids, not wanting to wake the sleeping dragon, relegated themselves to their bedrooms upstairs. Whatever mild amusement the game once provided—and she wasn't so sure it really had been a lick of fun—had waned.

The kids were stressed and had complained of being tired all day. And he... well, the morning's festivities showed what the game was doing to his senses, or what was left of them. Part of the problem, she suspected, was they were all eating crap, junk and side dishes and processed chemicals masquerading as food. They needed brain food, as her mom would say. Protein. Healthy fats. They were repeatedly riding the waves of blood sugar spikes and then crashing, so it was no wonder he was half out of his gourd already.

The cornucopia of alcohol and nicotine didn't help his marbles roll any straighter, either. He would have killed her today. She was sure of it. The look in his black, dead eyes told her he would have sliced and diced her without giving it a second thought. The kids, too, probably. In the end, she imagined him sitting perfectly content in the living room, smoking a cigarette, drinking a beer, and patting himself on the back for winning the game. *The goddamned game.*

They needed food, and they needed it tonight. She was going to have to make her way down into the basement while he snoozed and smuggle up enough meat to last a few days, and then sneak down and snag more for the weekend. She could be light as air and quiet as a mouse if she had to be. And she knew without a doubt that she had to be. If he woke up at any point during the clandestine food run, she knew this time, he'd kill her with that knife, and it wouldn't be quick.

She tucked an old steak knife under her shirt, taking care not to stab herself with it as she lingered in the doorway between the kitchen and the living room for what felt like hours. The house was unusually quiet for the middle of the day. Whatever the kids were up to, more than likely napping, they were doing it in silence. And other than the usual creaks and bangs the house made on its own, his rhythmic snoring was the only sound she could hear. Normally, the nasal hum of his snoring, which sounded more like the buzz of a chainsaw, irritated her to no end. But at this moment, it was the most beautiful music she'd ever heard, on par with "Moonlight Sonata" or "Rhapsody on a Theme of Paganini."

She moved like a ghost through the kitchen and into the living room, the den where the devilish dragon now soundly slept. The lids of his eyes fluttered as he slipped deeper and deeper into whatever depraved visions danced inside his head. But with every twitch and snore, her confidence grew stronger. Two spots creaked loudly when stepped on in the living room, and she knew exactly where they were. Without even realizing it, she maneuvered herself toward the basement door on the tips of her toes as though she were traversing a minefield somewhere in one of those desert countries with ridiculously hard to pronounce names.

Ten. Eleven. Twelve.

She counted each step, although she didn't know why. The Miller living room wasn't a sizeable area. It was rectangular, and his stupid oversized television damned near took up an entire wall. She didn't think he'd hung it securely, and these days, she wished the thing would just fall off the wall and crush him to death. But she knew—somehow, even then, she just *knew*—that she'd have to do it herself. It would be the fair maiden that must slay the fire-breathing dragon to save the village from fire and death. Something in her gut told her it was coming, and it wasn't just the voice. There was something else—her subconscious, maybe—telling her she would become a killer before the game was over.

Twenty-two. Twenty-three.

He snored loudly, a long one. The index finger on his right hand jerked several times and then stilled. The door was only a few feet away from her now. So near, and yet still so goddamned far away. A bead of sweat dribbled down her forehead and landed right in her eye. She wanted to rub it, but she dared not take her gaze off his sleeping form for even the millisecond it would take to wipe away the salty water burning her eye.

Twenty-eight. Twenty-nine.

She realized she was holding her breath and probably hadn't taken one since leaving the kitchen. *Thirty.* He ripped a noxious fart in his sleep. She could smell it instantly, foul and rotten.

Thirty-one. Thirty-two.

The door was within reach. He snored and moaned. The tips

of her fingers were all but touching the cracked wood as she took the final steps.

Thirty-three. Thirty-four.

The chipped gold-plated handle shone like the burning eyes of Medusa, the gorgon lady with snakes for hair whose gaze turned mortals into stone. She took a quick, quiet breath. A steady stream of sweat ran into her eyes, her underarms and forearms drenched with perspiration. Her hand shook as she wrapped her fingers around the cold metallic knob. She half expected it to burn her skin on contact, like a crucifix for vampires, but it only felt cold and rigid in her hand.

Sweat dripped off a lash into her eye. She could hear the *lub-dub* of her heart beating in her ears. A nervous gurgle bubbled and brewed in her belly. She twisted the knob gently to the right, and it turned the tiniest bit, then locked in place. Her heart skipped a beat. A surprised sigh slipped out of her mouth. On the love seat, his legs thrashed in a dream. She turned the knob to the left and then again to the right, but it only clicked in place.

Locked. It's locked, she thought. How had he locked the door? She didn't even know it could lock. Her hand gripped the knob tighter, and she twisted it again and again, expecting it to turn and the door to pop open. But it remained locked.

Dammit.

"What are you doing?" His voice and its calmness startled her.

She nearly screamed, but held it in. Her hand released the knob, and she put some distance between her and the door, which meant moving closer to him.

He was out of the chair now and on his feet. Alert and wide awake. "I said, what are you doing?"

"Oh." The words wouldn't come. She couldn't even think of a coherent sentence. There was nothing in her brain but a blank page. "Nothing, dear. Nothing."

He stepped toward her. "Funny. It doesn't look like you were doing nothing. Looks like you were up to something all right. Something mischievious. Something… illegal. You wouldn't be doing something illegal now, would you, dear?"

"Illegal?"

"Against the rules."

The fucking game. It's all about the fucking game.

"Oh." She thought about the steak knife under her shirt and burying it in the center of his chest, driving the tip of the steel blade through flesh and bone like the sword in the fucking stone. She could taste it. There was a heavy metallic taste in her dry mouth, and she assumed it was the taste of death. Not hers, but his. "I wasn't going to…"

"The basement is off-limits. Forbidden."

"I know," she said weakly as he stepped closer. She slipped a hand under her shirt and traced the handle of the knife with a finger. *Just like Ex-fucking-calibur.*

"Now, why would you wanna break the rules?"

"I…"

"You know what happens when you break the rules."

"P-p-p-punishment," she stammered, slipping two fingers on the wooden handle of the concealed knife.

"That's right. Punishment." He took a long step toward her, and she retreated until she was flush against the door. "Severe punishment."

He bridged the distance between them in an instant and slammed his palms against the door just beside her head. The bang reverberated in her ears, and she flinched despite her best effort to remain unaffected by his doings. Leaning his body against hers, they were now cheek to cheek, and the hair behind her right ear swayed with every exhalation he made. She felt the thing harden and grow in his pants, that awful thing between his legs. And she hoped he couldn't feel what she had stuffed under her shirt. "There's nothing down there, you hear? Nothing." He slammed a palm against the door to drive the point home. "Don't go down there. For anything. No matter what you might hear."

Hear?

"F-f-food. We need food, dear."

"Nah, we don't."

"We do. There's nothing left..."

"There's plenty of meat in the freezer."

"What?"

"The freezer. There's plenty of meat in the freezer. Did you even look in the freezer, you stupid, useless cunt?" She looked stunned, and he relished in it. " Well, did you?"

She shook her head slowly, and her cheeks burned bright red. She hadn't looked, and she hadn't thought to. There had been nothing in the freezer for two days but ice cube trays and a bag of cauliflower, which they all disliked. The kids would just as soon suck on an ice cube before they'd eat a single bite of "ghost broccoli."

"Say it, woman."

"No. I didn't look."

"Maybe you should before you do something stupid." He licked a trail of sweat dripping down the side of her cheek with his tongue. It felt like sandpaper against her skin. "Before you do something that might get you hurt." He let the last word linger a moment before pressing his lips gently on the center of her forehead. It was, even for him, an almost tender kiss, which took her by surprise. "Now go make me something for dinner. I'm fucking starved. And it better be good, you hear? Or I'll have to give you a spanking. A proper, bare-assed spanking."

The thought of him spanking her bare ass both revolted and terrified her, but she kept her brave mask on. "Yes, dear. I mean... sir," she breathed.

He removed his hands and backed away, smiling with each step. At the midpoint, he turned, showing her his back, and made for the stairs.

Like Ex-fucking-calibur, she thought.

But as she expected, the voice came back. *No, not yet.*

"Let's see what kinda trouble these kids are getting themselves into."

And with that, he lumbered up the stairs. It wasn't until he was gone from her sight that her muscles relaxed, the confident mask slipped off, and she melted to the ground in a wet puddle of tears. She lay there for a while, curled in a fetal position, oblivious to the muffled sounds coming from an upstairs bedroom. When she finally pulled herself together enough to stand, she peered into the kitchen freezer and was horrified to see it stocked with stacks of tinfoil-covered cuts of meat. The meat repulsed her, and she fought the urge to throw up what little food she had in the pit of her stomach.

She didn't know why the sight of the packs of meat wearing their shiny tinfoil dresses horrified her, but it did. A word kept repeating in her head like a skipping record. *Rotten. Rotten. Rotten.* Even though she hadn't tasted a morsel of the mystery meat, she couldn't stop thinking it was somehow spoiled. But the grumbling in her belly reminded her they had to eat. Best not to ask questions and just be thankful for the fresh bounty.

She threw a chunk of meat into a pan with a slice of butter, and it sizzled and hissed as the meat browned. She sprinkled it with salt, garlic, and pepper and hated to admit that it actually smelled good. No, better than good. It smelled delicious. Her stomach groaned in agreement. The heavenly scent of the cooking meat drowned out the endless chants of *rotten, rotten, rotten* that echoed in her head. For now, all she wanted to do, all she could think of, was eating every last morsel.

Little Pigs

The meat browned on the stove for twenty minutes. Even then, when she thought it was fully cooked, the meat was tender and juicy, a river of clear juice escaping as she poked it with her fork.

Now watching the kids devour the meat, shoveling forkful after forkful into their eager mouths, their faces shining with pure delight as the mystery meat made its trip from mouth to belly, she found it impossible to ignore the annoying pangs in her empty stomach. There wasn't much of a meal on her plate without the meat—some sorry, soggy asparagus spears and a couple of broccoli florets, neither of which she cared for that much.

Reluctantly, she plopped a small piece of the mystery meat into her mouth, just to have a little taste, and it filled her with a rush of flavors. She had planned not to eat the meat, for no other reason than to spite him, but it smelled so damned good.

It *was good. Delicious.* She had to admit it was probably the best meal she'd made, perhaps in her life. A groan erupted from her belly, an agonized *mooorrre,* and she took another bite. And then another. The bites became bigger until she too was shoveling the food into her mouth. She lowered her mouth to the plate and used her fork to push a pile of the juicy meat into her open cakehole. The fork shoveled the meat from the plate to her mouth so fast she could barely keep up, choosing to swallow instead of chew even the meatier chunks that passed through her lips.

She had to have more. She just *had* to. Her tongue lapped at the plate, weaving through the stray greens to slurp the slick layer of congealed juices the meat left behind. Noisily, her tongue darted around the plate as guttural, swine-like noises escaped her. It wasn't until she picked up the plate to lick it clean, spilling the last of the greens right into her lap, that she noticed a silence had come over the kitchen. Everyone stared at her with amazement on their faces, as though Sasquatch himself had just passed through the kitchen.

He smiled at her, both pleased and delighted with himself.

"What?" She placed the plate down gently. "What are you all staring at?"

"Somebody was hunnnngry! Soooooo-iieee! Pig! Pig! Pig!" He pushed up his nose and snorted like a pig into his plate. The kids cracked up at his shenanigans, egging him on. "Mommy's nothing but a filthy, stinking pig, isn't she, kids?" They laughed harder.

"Mommy, you're a pig." The young boy giggled into his hands.

The Girl squealed, "Oink! Oink! Oink!"

They continued to laugh and point, taking devilish pleasure in their amusement. Her face reddened with anger and embarrassment. He had done this. Him. It had all been him.

Oink! Oink! Oink! Soooo-iieee! Pig! Pig! Pig! Oink! Oink! Mommy, you're a pig!

She felt like Carrie in that old horror movie, the one where the bullies douse her in pig's blood at the prom.

It was there again, tingling in her skin just under the surface—the urge. There was a knife on the table. She could do it now while they were distracted by their own horseplay. Seize the knife, and cut their throats, one by one. Let them bleed out all over the table, gurgling in their blood while she had seconds and thirds.

Wouldn't that be funny? And she thought she understood then, at least some of it, why mothers killed their young and their sniggering, useless husbands.

They were still laughing, tears rolling down their flushed cheeks, when she stood up from the table and picked up the knife.

Oink! Oink! Oink! Sooooo-iieee! Pig! Pig! Pig!

He noticed her first. Or, more precisely, he noticed the blade first. He went to crack a smile, but something about the look in her eyes made him think better of that idea. He said nothing as she stepped out from the table. The kids, oblivious to the scene playing out around them, kept up with their relentless chants of *soooo-iiiee* and *oink, oink.*

"Whatcha gonna do with that now, huh?"

She took a step toward where he was seated at the end of the table like a king.

"You planning on using that thing? Or is it just for show?" He smiled now and stood up. "Come on, girl! Let's see what you're made of! Bring it right here! Right here!" He pounded a fist on his chest, in the spot where his beating heart resided. "Yeah, that's right. Let's see if you got what it takes to win this right here and now. Let us all see."

The kids abruptly muted their mouths, which fell open, aghast at what their eyes beheld.

Being more tortoise than hare, she moved around the table

at an even but deliberately slow pace. She was a patient person. Not quite with the patience of a saint, as they say, but she could be extremely patient when she had to be. Hadn't the game proven that? And there was also the voice. Hadn't she been patient thus far, waiting for the green light to end this madness once and for all? Not to mention the massive amounts of shit she'd already endured as the game played out to one inevitable conclusion—murder and death. But right then, the receptacle of their jeers and taunts, her patience had run dry.

She swung the blade wildly in his direction. It made a loud *whoooossshhhh* as she sliced through the air. Drawing back her arm, she cocked it and slashed at him with all her might. He was still far enough away from her that the blade missed, but it was enough for him to see that she meant business, not to maim, not merely to hurt, but to *kill*.

There was darkness in her eyes he'd never seen before. It was very much not the usual temperament he'd been accustomed to. She most definitely was not herself, like she'd fallen asleep and had been replaced by a pod person or some stupid shit like that. This was a new vision of her, one that ran on nothing but adrenaline and rage. And her tank was full. Very full.

"Why don't you just—" He tried to placate with his best greasy, used car salesman voice, but it was like throwing gas on a fire.

Her rage burned brighter as she slashed the blade at him. "Don't tell me what to do!"

"All right." He held up his hands. "All right. But would you look at the children? Please? You're scaring them."

She gripped the knife handle tighter and kept it pointed at him as she flicked her eyes to the kids. A second later, her gaze honed back on him. "You did this," she said softly. Her knuckles turned white as her fingers wrapped tighter around the handle. "*You.*"

He laughed nervously. Even in her agitated state, she could hear the nervous inflection in his usually biting laugh.

"Damn. The kids probably think you is gonna kill them like that crazy-ass bitch down in El Paso last year."

"Crazy-ass bitch," she said through gritted teeth. "You think I'm a crazy-ass bitch?"

Again, he laughed nervously.

She noticed he was sweating now, too. To her, he looked like a wiry worm wiggling on the end of a hook. And she just wanted to feed him to the fucking fishes and be done with him and the game.

"Nah. Nah. I didn't mean it like that. That Tejano bitch was crazy. I'm just saying, the way you is acting right now, the kids might get that idea. You might take a fancy to hurting them in your loco state."

"I'm not crazy. I'm not crazy. I'm not—"

"You sure is acting—"

"*Crazy!*" She swung the knife. This time, the blade struck him right in his forearm. It sliced through his shirt and skin as though they were warm butter. The torn fabric quickly reddened with blood. His eyes flashed open wide. One of the kids let out a high-pitched scream of fright. She couldn't tell which one, and, at that point, it didn't really matter. He winced in pain and jumped back a foot or two.

Now.

I can do it now.

He's on the ropes. He's on the run.

Kill him.

Cut his throat.

And then...

The voice cut her off, booming in her head. *NO. STOP THIS. NOW.*

She froze in place, holding the knife out in front of her. *But why? I don't understand. It can be over. Right now. We can end it. We can win.*

Again, it only said one word. *No.*

He saw the confused, glazed look on her face and pounced. The first punch caught her by surprise, and she dropped the knife. It clanged to the floor, and he kicked it across the room. He punched her face three more times as she howled in pain. Her hands flew to protect her face. Blood dripped down her chin. Both kids were screaming now. He punched her in the gut. Once. Twice. Three times. Then six times rapid-fire like a machine gun. It knocked all the air out of her. She gasped, sending a splatter of blood onto his face. He laughed as he watched her drop to the floor. She clutched at her stomach and her bruised ribs, screaming and hollering for him to stop as he kicked her mercilessly.

"Stoooooop iiiiiiit," she managed between kicks, but he only kicked harder. She turned her head to look at the kids and saw them standing there, watching him beat the living shit out of her and doing nothing. Somehow, she rolled herself into a ball and wrapped her limbs around her midsection like a protective shell, letting her arms and legs take the brunt of his relentless kicks.

She didn't really remember when he finally stopped, but he did—eventually. Her face was swollen, sore, and bloodied, and every part of her hurt. There were already countless bruises on her thighs and legs, not to mention the ones on her belly and back.

Time had passed, but she had no idea how much. The kitchen was empty save for a note tossed onto her mangled frame. *The dishes need washing.*

She wanted to cry, but no tears would come. Her shoulders shook as though going through the motions of a tearless sob. *Why? Why didn't you let me kill him? Whyyyyy?*

It would be a while before a reply came, but one finally did. And she found it gave her absolutely no comfort.

Trees are beaten by the wind, their leaves ripped by the rains. But still, they grow stronger. You must grow stronger to endure the storm that is coming.

Blood dripped from her nose into the sink. She turned on the water and washed a dish.

She had never felt so weak in all her life.

Alone Again, or... Not?

He left her alone that night. She didn't know where he slept or where he went, and she didn't care. It was better that way. She took a long shower to clean herself up, afraid if she took a bath, she wouldn't be able to get herself out of the tub. The water beneath her feet turned red as the shower's harsh spray chipped away at the blood that had dried in patches all over her body. An hour later, when the water had long turned cold and flowed clear, she limped out of the bathroom to get dressed and check on the kids.

The Boy had fallen asleep on the floor, reading a book. She slid a bookmark into place and closed the cover. The bedding was a mess, with the blanket and sheets ruffled as though there had been a commotion on the bed. *The kids like to wrestle.*

First, she tried to scoop him up into her tired, sore arms, but she knew there was no way she'd be able to lift him, let alone carry him to the bed in her condition. She tried to rouse him from sleep, but he resisted and seemed to only drift deeper into slumber the more she tried to shake him awake. Finally, she pulled a pillow and the blanket from the bed and placed them around The Boy's head and body. He barely stirred when she lifted his head to shove the pillow under it, nor when she wrapped him up in the fluffy blanket.

She went to click the lamp off beside the bed when something caught her eye on the bed—a bloodstain. It was small but obvious on the white sheet. She rubbed it with her finger and found it didn't smudge. The mark wasn't fresh, but something told her it wasn't exactly old, either.

An icy chill came over her as a thought she could not push away entered her mind.

I'm scared of the bad man.

She clicked off the light and crossed the hall. *Did he do this, somehow? Or...*

Across the hall, the young girl slept soundly in her bed. There was a tranquil look on her face, like she didn't have a care in the world.

As she climbed into her own bed, which she happily found empty, her thoughts dwelled on the bloodstain and how it might have gotten there. Had he been trying to tell her something when he'd said he was afraid of the bad man? Why was he scared of the bad man? Was the bad man hurting him? How?

And, most importantly, who was the bad man? *He*, her darling husband, was the obvious suspect. She was afraid of him, too. But what if it wasn't him? What if the bad man was someone else entirely?

Oh, no, she thought. *What if...*

A shiver swirled up and down her spine as the horrific thought became clear.

... there was someone else in the house?

Day Fifteen, Part One: Sour Suckers

The cable and Wi-Fi never came back on, so with the same five movies to watch on DVD, the natives were rightfully restless. The abrupt termination of the family's Wi-Fi proved not to be as big of a deal as losing their all-access cable subscription, since no one had access to a computer or electronic device. No one but him, that is.

Under "normal" circumstances, meaning the days before the game, losing the internet for even an hour sent the family into *Lord of the Flies* territory. And yet, somehow, they had all gone there willingly, to that place somewhere between the realms of sanity and insanity. He lacked what they commonly referred to as a *silver tongue*, but he turned into a regular P.T. Barnum in convincing them to play the game, which made *them* the suckers.

At first, the game seemed a reasonable enough way to pass the time while they waited. She was loath to admit she couldn't come up with a better plan, and she never in her wildest dreams imagined that the game would go on for more than a weekend, let alone degenerate into the shitshow it now was. While they had all chosen happy, smiling people to portray, he went full psycho, instead.

It was an odd choice, she thought, but understood why he

had gone that route. Crazy gave him freedom. You can't bottle crazy, and it can't be contained or ruled. If he'd walked through their front door fifteen days ago in a wool sweater and penny loafers, he wouldn't have been able to hit The Dog—*poor, poor Fido.* Or hit her. He probably also wouldn't have made her touch that awful thing between his legs. That wasn't the sort of thing nice guys asked nice girls to do.

Everybody loves a good girl. So, you make sure to be good, Ma—

She tied off that thought before it finished. She'd almost thought her name. For fifteen days now, she hadn't been that other person. It felt longer. She was losing her true identity, her soul, to this suburban mom she'd conjured out of nothingness. Not nothingness, entirely. Her "mom" was a bit Laura Ingalls Wilder mixed with Mary Shelley. An odd combination that seemed to work.

Her real life was receding into the shadows. He was already there, but she was still *here*, buried deep inside this role she'd been dealt. As long as she could remember something—anything—of that girl, everything could still be all right.

How much of their previous lives the kids still remembered, she didn't know for certain. They, too, appeared committed to their roles. While he was irredeemable, unwilling to separate himself from his character, the kids might be saved. *Might.*

If the game didn't go on much longer...

Things would never go back to the way they were before. How could they? Did he expect they'd just crown a winner and go back to their previous lives as if nothing had happened? Pretend he hadn't made her do those things? He was watching her undress all the time now. Openly. He didn't even try to hide his ogling or that hard thing in his pants. He sometimes rubbed it while she changed or stepped out of the shower, wrapped in nothing but a towel. She tried to be as modest as possible, but he was always there. Lurking around darkened corners or down the hall. A week ago, she swore he watched her from under the bedcovers while she got dressed in the morning.

Now, she sat in the kitchen, staring at the dead phone on the wall. It had all been about her. She knew that now, both in her heart and in her mind. There was no escaping or denying that truth, and the realization made her skin crawl. She felt *dirty*, like she'd been cutting grass under an August sun and sweating her little ass off. The feeling that she needed a shower was with her all the time now. And no matter how long she bathed, scrubbing her skin raw, she couldn't make herself clean. Somehow, she'd become the thing she'd always feared becoming—a bad girl. No. *A dirty girl.* She repulsed herself. And she imagined Laura Ingalls Wilder would similarly be disgusted.

The telephone still worked. It was just off the hook, as the kids said. All she had to do was pick up the receiver, hold down the switch hook, and wait for the dial tone to come back. She could call 9-1-1, but what would she tell them? How could she explain what was going on inside the house before she was found out? She could tell the police about Fido. *Poor, poor Fido.* That would certainly arouse their interest. They'd want to talk to her in person then. The kids, too. Surely the cops would see and end the game. Take him away, too, maybe.

Maybe...

She could call Grandma Miller. Even though she was on the other side of the country, Grandma Miller would do *something.* She'd come and put a stop to all of this. Punish him, too. All she had to do was tell Grandma Miller about the awful things he'd made her do, and she'd whoop his butt so raw he wouldn't be able to sit until September.

And there was nothing he could do about it. He was afraid of her. After all, the kids didn't call her "Old Ironside" for nothing. No one wanted to be on Grandma Miller's bad side. *That* would be a very, very bad thing indeed.

It was decided. When the time was right, when it was safe, she'd use the kitchen phone to call Grandma Miller. She reached across and pulled a cigarette out of the pack sitting on the table. Curiously, she held it to her nose and took a whiff.

She slipped the butt between her lips and lit it up. All bad girls smoked cigarettes. She coughed and choked as the poison filled her lungs for the first time. It took several tries, but eventually, she taught herself how to inhale and exhale the noxious gray smoke. The taste in her mouth wasn't as sour as she'd imagined. It wasn't pleasant, but not terrible, either. More pleasing than the flavor of her own blood, the smell was worse than the taste.

She wondered if she could blow a ring of smoke like she'd seen in the movies. Bad boys and bad girls could always do cool tricks with smoke, like blowing it through their nose so they look like a fuming dragon. The best she could manage was a thin cloud that was only somewhat circular.

By the time Grandma Miller arrives, I'm going to master this.

The coughing fit that followed should have convinced her to quit her newfound habit before it got the better of her.

Blackout

The power went off around noon. The kids were playing a lively game of Clue in the living room, and she didn't know where he'd gone off to. Most likely the basement, but she didn't know for sure. There was a loud clack, and then everything went off. It only took another second or two for the house to fall completely silent. The whir of the refrigerator died slowly, the hum of the cable box quieted, and the blades of the ceiling fan in the kitchen wound down until they stopped spinning. Then, all at once, every one of their wall unit air conditioners ceased blowing cold air, and no one needed reminding that it was a humid summer afternoon outside in the real world.

She was sitting on the edge of the bed, working out how she was going to get him out of the house to call Grandma Miller. The sudden clack startled her to her feet. She eyed the clock on the nightstand as its green LED lights pulsed one last time, as though it were a concluding gasp of life, and then watched the display go blank. By the time she moved to the door, she heard the unmistakable sound of him once more losing his shit.

He burst through the basement door and made his way into the living room with heavy, agitated-sounding footsteps. Each step sounded like a *fuck,* or a *shit,* or a *Jesus H. Fucking Christ.* "What the actual fuck is going on up here? What the hell did you kids touch?"

She hovered on the stairs, half out of the scene.

The kids shrugged. "Wasn't us," one of them said.

"We didn't do nothing," the other added.

"You musta. Electricity doesn't just go out," he said, enraged.

"Power's out upstairs, too, dear." She swallowed whatever spit she had in her mouth. "I mean, sir."

"Thank you, Captain Fucking Obvious." The kids laughed. She was not so easily amused anymore—if she ever had been. He fumbled with a bunch of switches throughout the first floor. "Power's out everywhere."

"Like, *everywhere* everywhere, sir? Or just everywhere in the Miller house?"

The kids stopped laughing and eyed him curiously. "Yeah, Daddy. Is it just us?"

He sighed and lumbered to the front window. "Let's have a look-see," he said, peering through the blinds in a way so as not to disturb them. The last thing they wanted—no, the last thing *he* wanted was for someone to know that the Millers were home. He thought he'd done an excellent job of convincing the outside world that the Millers were on vacation, and he didn't want to blow their cover now peeping through a slat in the blinds.

"What's going on out there?" she asked as she sat on a step. She wanted to look herself, to *see* the outside world again and remember there was a life beyond the claustrophobic walls of the Miller house and the game.

The stupid fucking game.

She longed to see a face that didn't belong to any of them. Hell, she'd even settle for Mrs. Garriga or that silly Mr.

Buchanan. Anyone would do.

"I can't see shit. It's quiet."

"But Daddy, I think I hear—"

"I mean, fucktwat, it's quiet as in everyone ain't standing on their front porches with their heads up their asses wondering what the Sam Hill is going on with the electricity. Just people out doing the usual summer shit."

Summer shit. That was what she wanted to be doing—running through an open hydrant, sunning in the yard, or reading at Jones Beach with her friends. The carefree things you take for granted. The greatest sin of man is that he always thinks there will be more time; time enough to do everything he's ever dreamed of. Only, that's not the way of the world. We stay in when we should go out. We say no when we should say yes. And why? Because we can do it tomorrow. Or next week. Or next year. Now, sitting on a step in the Miller house, feeling the first trickle of perspiration trailing down her back, she wondered if she'd ever get to do any of the things she'd planned to do with her life.

"Dear... I mean, sir?"

"Huh?" He barely seemed interested in her.

"I know you probably don't want to hear this right now, with the power crisis and all—"

"It ain't a crisis, for fuck's sake. It's a problem. And every problem has what, kids?"

"A solution," they squealed in unison.

"Right." She took a breath, preparing for his reaction, and continued. "Well, whatever *this* is, if we don't keep the meat cold, it will be a crisis."

His head whipped around to look at her. The blinds rattled against the windowpane. "Oh shit. Shit. Shit. Shit. *Shiiiiit!*"

129

Then an idea came to her through a blanket of muddled thoughts. The idea wasn't hers—at least, she suspected it wasn't *entirely* hers. The voice suggested *ice.*

"Why don't you go get some ice? Maybe a cooler? That way, the meat will keep until the power comes back on." She smiled warmly at him. *Got to get him out of the house. Call Grandma Miller. Get him out.* "What do you think, sir?"

"You know, even though you is a stupid cunt, that's not a half-bad idea."

Stupid cunt. I'll show you, turd. I'm going to win this game. "What if you take the kids with you? They could probably use an outing. I think we're getting a little stir *crazy.*" She emphasized the word "crazy" but it went right over his head.

"Those fuckers? Why the hell would I wanna go ahead and do that? I'm no babysitter. That's woman's work, *woman.* And I'm a man. A man!"

"I understand, dear. But they've been cooped up for two weeks now. I think they could use some fresh air."

He guffawed. "Fresh air?"

"A change of scenery." She stared right at him, willing him to accept her idea. *Take them and go.* "It would be good for them." *The game.* "You know, so they can keep on playing."

All at once, the kids jumped to their feet and tugged at his shirt. He gave her a suspicious look. The kind that said *I know you're up to somethin', you stupid cunt, but I don't know what. Yet.*

"One of you." He eyed her to gauge her reaction. Her face was cold steel. "I'll take one of you."

"Me! Me! Me!"

"I'll take..." he began and pretended to debate the merits of each child. But she knew which of the kids he'd pick. "You." And he pointed to the girl.

"Yay! I win! I win!"

"I didn't wanna go, anyway." The young boy pouted and plopped his rear on the step below hers. She tussled his hair and wrapped him in a gentle bear hug.

"It's all right. Let them go," she whispered in his ear.

The Boy looked up at her, and she planted a kiss on his forehead, which made him smile.

"Where's mine?" he said from the bottom step.

Right here. I got yours right here, asshole.

She withdrew her arms from The Boy and descended the stairs slowly, step by step, until she was about halfway down and they stood face to face. For the first time since the game began, she noticed the sharpie mustache was gone. There was only a faint outline above his lip where the mock 'stache had been scrawled. She sat down with deliberate precision. "What happened to your mustache?"

He grinned at her, opening the front door. "Shaved it off. Come on, kid."

Perched on the stairs, she looked at the world outside longingly. The cloudless sky never looked so blue—like an ocean she wanted to swim in. Dive in, and swim away. A slight gust of wind swept in and lapped at her legs, teasing her. *God, it feels good. So good.* She hadn't realized how much she'd missed it all and how much she hated being cooped up inside all day, every day. The Miller house had become a cage, and she was the nightingale trapped behind its bars.

He gave her a knowing wink and was about to usher The Girl outside when she had the most awful thought.

"No! Wait!" She jumped as though her ass had caught fire and hurled herself down the stairs, taking two steps at a time until she reached the bottom. Out of breath and sweating, she said to the child, "You need his permission! Ask his permission to go outside!"

The expression that washed across his face told her everything she needed to know. For once, she was one step ahead of him. Now she just needed to stay ahead.

"Ask him!"

"Daddy, can I go outside with you, even if it's really against the rules?"

He waited before saying anything, pondering. Eventually, he gave in. He'd been defeated—for now, anyway. "Of course, you have my permission to accompany me on this super-important mission." He raised his head and squinted his eyes, even though there was no sun in them. "The rules still apply to everyone else, though."

She laughed nervously. "Of course, dear. Sir. Dear, sir."

"Because if anyone goes getting any bright ideas, there will be cons-eee-quences. Mucho cons-eee-quences. Comprende?"

She nodded, afraid her voice would betray her plans to call Grandma Miller.

"All right, then. We are agreed. See ya'll later." He herded the child through the open doorway onto the porch. He took one step over the threshold before he stopped and turned back to say, "Do something with yourself while I'm out, okay? You look busted. Don't look busted when I get home." He eased the rest of his body through the doorway and pulled the door shut. The wooden frame rattled, and then a second later, the myriad of metal locks clicked into place, one by one, until one half of the Miller family was again locked in. He stood there on the porch, behind the front door in the real world, for a minute or two.

She wondered if anyone saw him leave. That Nosey Nellie, Mrs. Garriga, was probably watching. But there was one thing about Mrs. Garriga she knew for certain—she was all talk, and didn't have the balls to do anything. The longer she let things go, the more juicy a tale the old bitty got to tell to her friends later.

She imagined he was lingering on the porch to see if she tried something stupid, like running through the front door twenty seconds after he had. Part of her wanted to do just that—get the keys, break the damned locks if she had to, and escape the Miller house, forcing the end of the game. Let him return to an empty house and wonder where they'd gone. But what about the young girl? What would happen to her once he realized the house and the game had been abandoned?

Poor, poor Fido.

No, she wouldn't run. Not yet. He was likely watching the house from up the street. And she knew he'd chase her down and kill her in the middle of St. Augustine Place if he caught her trying to run. Or worse, kill the kids for *her* folly.

No, she decided as she listened for his heavy, plodding footsteps crossing the porch and going down the drive. Calling Grandma Miller was not only her best option but her *only* option. She just prayed the old woman was home and not sitting in front of a slot machine somewhere on the Vegas Strip.

Summertime, and the Living's Not Easy

"I'm hot," the young boy whined.

"I am, too." The power had only been off for fifteen minutes at most, and the house already felt twenty degrees warmer. It hadn't gotten that hot so quickly, but she knew it would soon enough if the power didn't come back on. The small drip of sweat down her back had turned into a flowing river. She felt sticky all over. Every stitch of clothing hugged and squeezed her slick skin. "Why don't you take a shower?"

"But, Mommmyyy! I'm hot! Why would I take a shower if I'm hot?"

"A cold shower, dummy."

"A cold shower? Why would anyone wanna take a cold shower?"

She knew of a few reasons. At school, leering boys would sometimes joke about needing a cold shower after "Double-D Debbie" jiggled down the hall. And while she wasn't entirely sure why they needed a cold shower, she assumed it had something to do with the things between their legs that magically sprung to life in Debbie's presence. "To cool yourself down, silly."

"Oh. Yeah." The young boy giggled.

"Go on and try it. I bet you'll like it."

"Okay. But, Mommy?"

"Yes?"

"I'll be back," The Boy said in a robotic, lifeless voice and then disappeared up the stairs.

The bathroom door slammed shut, followed by the sound of the shower faucet turning on. *Have to make it quick. Pick up the phone and call Grandma Miller before he gets back. I don't know how long he'll last in the shower.*

She held the receiver to her ear and tapped the hook switch several times until she heard the hum of a dial tone in her ear. There was a steady tone, and then five fast tones, followed by a steady tone again. *Messages. There were messages.* She stared at the keypad. It had been so long since they had any messages to retrieve that she couldn't remember the password.

1-1-1-1? No.

0-0-0-0? No.

6-9-6-9? No.

1-2-3-4. Bingo, she was in.

The electronic attendant said, "Hello. Your mailbox is full. You have... twenty-nine new messages... and... six saved messages. Main menu. Press one to hear new messages. Press two to hear saved messages. Or press pound to exit the system."

She pressed one.

"First new message. 'Hey, yeah, Bill. Todd Rudledge here. Just wanted to see if you've given any more thought to switching to BX Health. The coverage looks comparable, and the rates are competitive. Anyway, give me a call when you're back from vacation. Bye now.'"

Press one to replay message. Press two to save message. Press three to erase message. Press four to skip to the next new message.

Or press pound to exit to the main menu.

She nervously pressed two. He might want to hear the message later when the game was over. "Message saved."

"Next new message. 'Denise, hiiiiiiiiii. It's Joanne. Joanne Garriga from next door. I know you're on vacation, but I wasn't sure if we were supposed to collect your mail. Mr. Buchanan says it's piling up over there. I can hold it, no problem. I guess if you hear this, just give me a buzz, okay? Okay.'"

This time after the instructions, she pressed three.

Message erased.

"Next new message. 'Good morning, William Miller. I'm calling about the warranty on your—'"

She didn't need to hear the entire message before pressing three.

Next new message.

"... press one to make a payment on your Riverside Cable account now. Press two to make a payment arrangement. Or press three to speak to a billing specialist. Press nine to repeat these options."

She tapped three.

Message erased.

"Next new message. 'Yeah, Bill. It's Mike. Not sure if you're checking emails on vacation, but we really need to talk about the Hillings account ASAP. I know you're technically out, but please call me at the office or at home. This can't wait until next week.'"

She hit two.

Message saved. Next new message.

"Yeah, Bill. Mike again. Call me."

She didn't wait for the attendant to complete their menu of options before she pressed two.

Message saved. Next new message.

"Yeah, Bill. It's Mike. Again. Where the fuck are you, man? We need to talk. Call me. I'll try your cell. Again. Okay."

She pressed two.

Message saved.

The uneasy feeling in her stomach grew stronger with each new message. Mike sounded concerned. *Angry* and concerned. Mike had no idea where Billy was.

Next new message.

"Your shutoff has been scheduled due to nonpayment. To make a payment by phone and avoid interruption, press zero to speak to a representative."

She swallowed hard and pressed two.

Message saved. Next new message.

"Bill. It's Mike. This is serious. Where are you? Call me. Today. I mean it."

She tapped two.

Message saved. Next new message.

"Hello! It's Grandma Miller. Just wanted to see how everyone is doing. I know you're planning your staycation thing this week, but I haven't heard from you in a few days, and I'm getting worried. Give an old lady a call, won't you, Billy? Love you! Mwah!"

Grandma Miller, she cried as she pressed two.

Message saved. Next new message.

"Seriously, Bill. If I don't hear from you by the end of the day, you're fired."

She wanted to throw up.

Message saved. Next new message.

"Hi, it's Joanne again. From next door. Mr. Buchanan said you stopped the mail. There was some overflow, so I have it here whenever you guys get back. Alrighty. Enjoy your vacation!"

Message erased.

That's why Mr. Buchanan never came back around, she realized at once. He must have snuck out to fill in the form or... used one of the confiscated devices to do it online before the internet got shut off.

Next new message.

"Your desk and office have been boxed up, Bill. You can pick your stuff up at the front desk whenever you pull your head out of your ass. Your severance will be sent separately. Good luck, man. It's a tough market out there. What the fuck were you thinking?"

Message saved.

Billy had been fired. Did he know? Where was he? If Mike didn't know, then who did? She thought of the note he'd read before they'd all agreed to play the game. Now she wondered if Billy had written it at all.

Next new message.

"Billy? It's your Ma. Call me, okay? I'm worried. Mwah."

Message saved. Next new message.

"It's urgent that we speak with you today. Your shutoff has been scheduled due to nonpayment. To make a payment by phone and avoid interruption, press zero to speak to a representative."

Message saved. Next new message.

"Hello? Is anybody home? It's Grandma Miller. Billy? Where is everybody? Denise? Mary? Junior? Toby? Justin? Alex? Hello? Will somebody please call me back? Anybody? It's Grandma Miller. Mwah!"

Message saved. Next new message.

"This is Go-TEL. We need to discuss the past due balance on you cellular—"

Message saved. Next new message.

There was some sobbing before, "I'm sorry, man. I am. But where the hell are you? Call me. It's Mike. We'll work something—"

Message saved. Next new message.

"Billy, Denise... I'm coming out there." It was Grandma Miller again. "You've made me do this. You're not answering any of my calls or messages. All I have to say is you'd better be dead when I get out there. Otherwise, I'll kill you both myself for ignoring me. Hope all is well. See you in a day or so. Love you. Mwah!"

She let the full message play and waited for the timestamp. It was two days ago. That meant Grandma Miller was due to arrive any time now, if she hadn't gotten into town already. But she hadn't heard anyone at the door. The buzzer hadn't so much as made a peep since Mr. Buchanan rang it a bit excessively.

She knew Grandma Miller wouldn't stop at a hotel or to eat, especially if she thought her Billy was in trouble. She'd probably come with the cavalry, breaking down the door and everything. At least, she hoped Grandma Miller would bring help. No matter how sturdy she appeared, the woman was almost ninety-five freaking years old. One good slip and fall could do her in. Still, showing up and being there might be enough. He feared her. Hell, everyone did. He'd shit a load of bricks if he heard her at the door.

Next new message.

She hung up, held down the hook switch, and then released it. The voice attendant's monotone voice had been replaced by the hum of the dial tone. Carefully, she placed the receiver on top of the phone, just as he had done. She kept fidgeting with it, moving it this way and that until it looked picture-perfect. If she couldn't spot the difference, he sure as shit wouldn't be able to, either.

Okay, she thought. *She's coming. Grandma Miller is coming. Help is coming. This will all be over soon. Probably today. She'll come, and everything will be okay. I'll tell her about Fido. Poor, poor Fido. Maybe we can still find him. Grandma will get the power and internet back on. We can call Mr. O'Hare at Daddy's job. Go to the Grub Mart and get some real food. Yes. That's what we'll do. Everything is going to be all right.*

Relief washed over her. The muscles in her shoulders finally dropped and the ball of angst that had moved into her stomach vanished. She smiled then. And why not? Grandma Miller was coming. She might even be here before he got back with the ice. And my, won't he be surprised when he walks in and sees her scowl? She saw it so clearly in her head and tried not to laugh aloud as she pictured the look of absolute horror on his face when he walked in and saw Grandma Miller. Hands on her roomy hips, foot tapping a mile a minute.

But what she didn't know was that she was on the smooth part of the roller coaster before it gets bumpy and climbs higher and higher into the heavens—that's when the fear takes over and panic sets in. Staring down at the drop from the top of the world, knowing any little miscalculation could derail the whole goddamned ride and kill everyone instantly. As with any good thrill ride, there would be screams. Lots of screams to come. And yes, there would be blood. She just entered the home stretch. The clock began ticking down to the end.

"Mom?"

The young boy entered the kitchen while she was lost in her

granny rescue fantasy. *Everything is going to be all right.*

"Mom?"

Everything is going to be all right.

"Mom!"

Everything is going to be—

"*MARY!*" the child finally screamed.

She spun around, slapped out of her daze by the sound of her name. Her true name. The panic returned instantly. *The child has broken the rules. Broken character. There will be punishment. Maybe for us both. He mustn't find out. Help is coming. Everything will be all right. If we can just—*

"Mary," the child cried, holding up a hand. "I'm bleeding, Mary. Why am I bleeding?"

Mary looked at the young girl no longer pretending to be a boy and saw the fresh blood smeared across her fingers. And then she looked lower, between the girl's legs, and saw the red-stained cotton undies she wore. The girl, Mary's younger sister, had gotten her first period.

"Oh no, Alex," Mary cried, softly at first and then full-on sobbing. "Oh, no." She ran to comfort Alex, who had begun to cry as well. Mary threw her arms around Alex and rocked her gently side to side. The child thought she was dying, slowly bleeding to death from her "hoo-hoo."

"I don't wanna die, Mary! Help me!"

Mary laughed a little, recalling how she also thought she would exsanguinate through her vagina when she had her first menstrual cycle only a few years earlier. "You're not going to die, silly. Come on. Let's get you cleaned up. I'll show you what to do."

She reluctantly broke their embrace, forcing Alex to separate from her, and wiped the tears streaming down the young girl's cheeks. Mary was about to take Alex by the hand and lead her back upstairs to the bathroom to tell her all about the wonderful world of becoming a woman when she realized an awful truth. *He might get home before Grandma Miller arrives. Alex* can't *have her period. In the game, Alex is a boy, and boys don't menstruate. She'll be breaking character if she has her period. Breaking the rules.*

"Alex?"

"Yeah, Mary?"

"You can't tell Junior."

The Second Interlude

Cast-Iron Cassie boarded the stuffy Delta 747 at five fifty on Saturday morning, several days after initially deciding to fly east and one day after leaving her last message on the Miller's electronic voicemail. She hated leaving messages because she knew people—sometimes the Millers—sat by their devices, screening their calls.

Why have a telephone if you're not going to answer the darned thing? It's just rude, she would say when she finally got her Billy on the line, and he'd try to soothe the scorned old woman with some fanciful story about running errands or running the kids somewhere, but, somehow, she *knew*. Cast-Iron Cassie always knew. That woman could smell bullshit from twenty-five hundred miles away over antiquated copper wires.

She also hated the sound of her own bassy, throaty voice. Mary sometimes saved the messages just to play them back when she visited around the holidays. *Oh, Grandma, you're so funny,* Mary would cackle as Cassie cringed, listening to the sound of her own pre-recorded voice. Mary was a good kid, one of the best. This was her only vice, so Cassie let it slide. Besides, she knew Mary adored her, and it was all in good fun.

Now, if it had been Junior pulling the playback shenanigans, she would have whopped that boy's behind until it was redder than a lobster's ass. And she would've enjoyed that. Junior was no Mary. If Mary was the saint of the family, then Junior was its resident sinner. And Junior's proclivity to darkness only worsened when he started listening to Dakotah Dark, the Swedish occult rock star who performed a black mass onstage—and not long after, disappeared in Berlin after a supposed car crash in the early eighties. Rumors persisted that Dark had conjured something on that stage. Something unholy.

There was *always* something off about Junior. Even before the music.

He wasn't the oldest of the Miller brood. Justin was the firstborn, but even he was afraid of Junior.

What Cassie didn't know was that more often than not, Justin would give in and just do whatever Junior wanted, like spying on Mary in the shower through a peephole he'd dug into the wall or browsing the web for graphic torture videos. They'd watch the latest uncensored ISIS beheading, or drug mules being gutted by the cartel. The stuff gave Justin nightmares and Junior an erection.

Junior was obsessed with death as a kid. Rather than put a struggling insect or animal out of its misery, Junior liked to watch them die... as slowly as possible. A bunch of kids got caught throwing rocks and sticks at some stray cats near the train yard near St. Augustine Place. Junior was not among those detained, but Cassie was not only sure that Junior had been there, but that he'd been the ringleader. But Billy stuck up for Junior, defended the boy as usual. *You got him all wrong, Ma. Junior's a good kid and would never do something like that. Not in a million years.* She heard his words in her head as though he were saying them now. *Junior's a good kid.*

In the animal world, some mothers ate their young. And there had been plenty of times since Junior had been born that Cassie had wished to the Almighty that Denise had devoured that infant. She'd been around long enough to know how to spot rotten fruit, and Junior was rotten to the core. And that was the one thing no parent, no matter how hip, wanted to hear.

I'm sorry, dear, but your kid is a bit of an asshole. More tea?

No parent took that news well. Most of the time, an asshole kid meant asshole parents. But that was not the case with Junior. Billy and Denise were wonderful parents and good people, although Cassie would never admit either. No point in giving anyone a swelled head.

She had bought a seat in economy, knowing full well she'd get an upgrade at the airport, which she did. Now she sat in the window seat of the last row in first class, chewing at her fingers—something she hadn't done since she was a teenager. For a brief time, around the onset of puberty, Cassie suffered severe bouts of anxiety and would sometimes gnaw her fingers almost right down to the bone.

She wouldn't do that this morning. The sour-faced flight attendants, especially the one with the just-rolled-out-of-bed hair, scuttling up and down the five aisles in first class wouldn't appreciate a bleeder on their flight.

It would take five and a half hours to fly from Harry Reid International Airport in Vegas to JFK in New York, so she would have to find some way to keep her mind occupied for the duration. Otherwise, Cast-Iron Cassie Miller might just go mad as her mind conjured a million and one different scenarios to explain why Billy wasn't responding to her. They ranged from the fantastic—aliens, of course, it was aliens—to the probable—they were all dead.

Almost all. Everyone but Junior.

When the feeling first hit her, Cassie couldn't even fathom the idea that her Billy could be dead. There was nothing more awful for a parent than to outlive their child. And whenever she imagined what the last moments on her deathbed might look like, her Billy was right there at her side, holding her hand and stroking her hair. A life without her Billy wasn't a life worth living at all. She liked her grandkids fine and all, even loved some of them. But Billy was all she was living for. That was why, at nearly ninety-five years old, she was flying over two-thousand miles on a whim. Maybe not a whim, but a hunch. One hell of a hunch.

The plane touched down on the tarmac in New York with a rickety skid half an hour ahead of schedule—a first. Cassie plowed through the bustling terminal, pushing her roller bag like a people mower. She threw shade to anyone who thought the old gal needed assistance or, worst of all, a ride in that embarrassing glorified golf cart. Cast-Iron Cassie would sooner crawl than be paraded around the airport in that jalopy.

Outside, her driver waited, a middle-aged Asian fellow with thick round glasses and a head full of salt-and-pepper hair, holding a sign that read "C. Miller." She studied him for a moment and decided that he was driving to make ends meet. Hell, everybody had two or three jobs these days, despite the supposedly "booming" economy. By the looks of him, Cassie figured the ends didn't quite meet, and he didn't own a house or even rent an apartment but slept in his car.

"That's me," she said, pointing to the chicken scratch on the sign.

"Good morning. Welcome to New York, Miss Miller. First

time?"

"Let's cut to the chase, sonny boy. My family is in a bad way, so I'm kind of in a hurry. So don't think me rude if I nix the pleasantries and just get down to the business at hand. How fast can you get me to the Bronx?"

The driver smiled. "I like a woman who knows what she wants. GPS says fifty-six minutes." Cassie frowned. "I'll have you there in forty-five—tops," he said with a wink. The driver reached across to take her roller bag.

"No, it's all right. Thank you. I can do it."

She hurled the roller bag into the trunk of his Chevy Cruze, and moments later, they were on their way.

He played the radio softly, some easy-listening adult contemporary music station. By the time they arrived at St. Augustine Place, precisely forty-three minutes later, Cassie had been subjected to Neil Diamond, Kenny G, Celine Dion, and, worst of all, Josh Groban. She practically jumped out of the car when they pulled up in front of the Miller house to escape the mega reverb on the latter's already warbly vocals.

Cassie slipped the driver a crisp fifty-dollar bill and a warm smile. He returned the smile and asked if Cassie wanted him to wait, "just in case." It was probably a good idea, but she shook her head, assuring everything would be fine. She thanked him again and watched him return to his car and drive off.

Everything will be all right. You'll see, Cassie repeated to herself, hoping she'd start to believe it. She *needed* to believe it. No matter what she found on the other side of that door, no matter what fate the Millers had been dealt, Cast-Iron Cassie needed to believe that, somehow, everything could still be all right.

She dragged the roller bag behind her, no longer as determined to reach her final destination as she had been less than an hour ago in JFK. Every fiber of her being throbbed with angst. The impulse to gnaw her fingers returned, but she fought hard to resist. There was no sense in stopping to have a light bite now when the house was but one hundred feet away. Then seventy-five feet away.

Fifty.

Thirty.

Twenty.

Ten.

And then, finally, Cassie stood on the porch with a nervous lump in her throat. She stood stiffly, listening for any signs of life coming from behind the door. But as she expected, the house remained silent as a graveyard, and standing there made her equally uneasy.

A subtle odor radiated all around the house. Most people wouldn't even detect it, but she had the nose of a bloodhound. Cassie knew that smell well. The scent tickled her nostrils when she'd visited friends in hospice. It was the distinct foul stench of death.

Cast-Iron Cassie wanted to retch right there on the porch, lean over the railing and let it all fly out of her mouth. But she didn't. Whatever was working its way up, she swallowed back down. She eyeballed the mailbox. There were two "Sorry we missed you" notices from a parcel delivery service. The first one was from last Thursday, and the second one was from yesterday. It had been stamped with *Final Delivery Attempt*. She wondered why the delivery person wouldn't just leave the parcel with a neighbor, but then she recalled Billy didn't trust the neighbors not to open up and rifle through their packages. This was something he'd picked up from her, the paranoia, but she saw now the folly of such thinking. *Stupid, stupid boy.*

With fingers that shook as though they were being zapped by ten thousand volts of electricity, she pressed hard on the buzzer and held it down for a good five seconds. Inside, the bassy boom of the electronic buzzer wailed and echoed throughout the house. Cassie released the buzzer, but her fingers hovered over it at the ready.

She didn't know what she had expected to hear or what might happen, but nothing stirred within the walls of the Miller house—not even a mouse. No familiar sound of Alex, Justin, or Mary scrambling to answer the door first. Cassie didn't hear *anything* inside the Miller house.

Sweat gathered around her forehead, threatening to spill. With the time change from the west coast to the east coast, it was now mid-afternoon on a scorching summer's day. She then noticed the lame air conditioner embedded in the front wall of their living room.

Perhaps it's dead.

The blinds were drawn, too. Not just the ones in the front window, but all of them. Cassie licked her suddenly dry lips, trying to moisten the cracked skin, but her tongue had also dried.

She pressed down on the buzzer, holding it in place this time for ten seconds. Then she released it and immediately pressed it down again for fifteen more seconds before letting up. Then once more for damned close to a minute. Cassie was sure the entire block could hear the annoying buzz of the Miller's doorbell. It was loud enough to wake the dead, but she didn't care. Let someone try to complain. See where that got them. The old gal could still pack one hell of a wallop. She'd knocked Peter Pastore's dentures clear across the frozen foods aisle for getting too handsy just last month.

Reluctantly, Cassie removed her hand from the plastic button. She tried the knob, but the door was locked. "Hello? It's Grandma Miller. Is anybody home?" she called out in a resounding voice that pierced the wooden door. When no reply came—not that she expected one—Cassie pounded on the door. The frame rattled with each smash of her fist, but the Miller house remained eerily silent.

She fumbled at her key ring and then remembered she had taken the keys to the Miller house off last December when Billy changed the locks and had "forgotten" to send her a new set. Cassie thought for a moment, then abandoned her roller bag and headed around the back of the house. There was a cellar door. Billy usually kept a key for that door under a rock, just in case of an emergency. And this, she reasoned, most assuredly qualified as an emergency.

The grass in the yard was overgrown and tinged with brown and yellow patches. Bags of garbage spilled out of the plastic bins. One looked as though some critter had a field day with its contents. The silver padlock on the shed door shone under the blistering summer sun. The children's playhouse was boarded up, much in the same fashion as the main house itself.

She never did see the need for it. The house was roomy enough for the kids to play in, and they were all teetering on being too old to have tea parties and play dress up in it, anyway. She'd tried to talk Billy into tearing it down last Christmas, but he was proud of it. Said the kids still loved it, and maybe they didn't have tea parties anymore, but they could use it to read or play games or just decompress away from parental eyes. Cassie still didn't understand the allure, but she dropped the issue. Staring at it now, sweating like a pig on a summer's afternoon, she realized just how much she hated that playhouse.

The key was exactly where Billy had left it—under a realistic hunk of plastic molded and colored to look like a slab of shale. She held it in her palm for the longest time, preparing herself to face whatever lay on the other side of the cellar door.

Okay, Lord. I know we haven't done much conversing in some years, but please let me be wrong about all this. Please. I'm begging you. Whatever it is, whatever he's done, take me instead, you hear me now? Take me. Just leave my Billy be, okay? Do we understand each other? Do we have a deal?

But the Almighty, much like the Miller house itself, said nothing.

She slipped the key into the keyhole and turned it to the right. The cellar door unlocked and popped open. Cast-Iron Cassie stepped inside, and even before her eyes could adjust to the dark, she screamed.

It was the smell that got to her. She didn't need to see anything to know the smell of feces and rotting flesh. Something had died in the cellar. She felt unsteady on her feet, the pungent odor of death rattling her old bones.

Damn you. I thought we had a deal, Lord.

Cassie stepped further into the cellar. With the sunlight streaming in through the open door and her eyes adjusting to the change in light, she slowly began to see. And then her brain made sense of what her eyes were seeing, or tried to, as best it could without breaking.

There stood a massive cage, the kind used to kennel dogs, but the Millers didn't have a dog. Denise was allergic. Alex, too. And, dear Lord, what was that *inside* the cage? There was something inside the cage, right? It wasn't a trick of the shadows but something three-dimensional, something alive

151

or something that once was alive. *Dear Lord.* She saw it move.

Cassie Miller screamed to the heavens above.

The thing, whatever it was, moved again. It opened an eye and gazed at her. She heard its labored, heavy breathing. The thing in the cage groaned as if caught in a trap.

Cassie stepped closer, slowly, but with fervor. *What in dear god is that?*

The beast, covered in its own vomit and shit, tried to sit up. She screamed again, not meaning to, but she couldn't help it. For the first time in her long life, Cast-Iron Cassie wasn't in control.

The thing in the cage vomited with agonizing heaves. The smell was so foul, so awful; it was unlike anything Cassie had ever smelled before. It was as if the beast was throwing up death itself, expelling its own life with every hurl and heave.

She covered her nose and walked closer to it. *Oh, dear Lord, have mercy.*

The thing let out a sickening gasp and hurled a long steady stream of brown and yellow bile and vomit. The sight of it made Cassie want to heave herself, but she continued to move closer to the cage and the beast that lay trapped inside.

"Helllp meeeee," Cassie thought she heard the beast murmur between upchucks. She knew the voice. She knew it well. But it couldn't be. There was no possible way on god's green earth that this, this *thing*, was him.

No. She was mistaken. She had to be.

But it spoke again, more clearly this time, "Helllp me."

And then she saw it.

Saw *him.*

Her grandson, Justin, locked in a cage like a dog.

All she could do was scream as tears ran down her cheeks.

"Help. Me," Justin groaned. "Dear god, please help me."

Cassie reached for the latch on the cage door when suddenly the cellar door slammed shut. She spun around on her heels, and even caressed by shadow, Cassie instantly recognized the shape in the darkness.

"Junior," she said with disgust.

Cassie thought the boy smiled at her but couldn't be sure because the next thing she knew, she was struck across the face—*hard*—by a cast-iron skillet. The taste of blood filled her mouth.

She swallowed a mouthful of spit and blood, along with several teeth. Some were hers and some were falsies. He smashed her face again, breaking her nose with a horrendous *crack!*

Blood streamed down her face, staining her blouse. She groaned and fell to a knee. The skillet smashed into the left side of her face. The bones in her cheek and eye socket broke apart like crackers. Cassie struggled to protect her face with her hands, but he swiped the skillet at them with ferocity. Three of her fingers twisted and bent in the wrong direction. She howled as pain rocked her body once more.

Then he was gone. Cassie could only see clearly through one eye, and it couldn't find his form in the dark cellar. But he was still there. She knew it. A second later, the skillet hit the ground with a clatter.

He's behind me.

Cassie turned on her knee and shrieked as it came toward her. There was no time to move, nothing she could do to fend it off. This was it. This was how she was going to go.

Junior ran at her, pushing the Christmas reindeer. Its antlers tore through her flesh and bone with ease and popped out the other side with a loud, bloody splat. The old woman choked on her blood, thinking, *I always hated that boy.*

Junior surveyed his handiwork, tears streaming down his face from laughing so intensely.

The thing in the cage, which had once been Justin and later became Fido in the game, sobbed into his hands.

"Oh, shit. I guess Grandma really did get run over by a reindeer." Junior chuckled before bursting into song.

Day Fifteen, Part Two: The Witching Hour

She saw him right away and screamed.

"Oh, my lord! What happened?" Mary cried. They'd returned with the ice several hours ago, and then Junior went out again for more than an hour, but this time, he didn't say why. His face had grown pale, and he got up from the sofa and went out the door. *There was someone at the door. The doorbell. It rang over and over and over again. And that made him nervous, scared even, even though he'd said not to worry about it. But* now he was covered in blood from head to toe. Mary couldn't help but wonder whose blood Junior took a bath in.

She ran to meet him at the door, nearly patting him down like she'd seen countless times on that awful reality show *COPS*. "What happened? Are you hurt?"

Junior brushed her off. "Nah, I'm good. It's not my blood. You should see the other guy," he said with a wicked little wink.

What other guy?! she thought. *Who did Junior tussle with?* Were they the one ringing the doorbell earlier? If so, she hoped they'd come around looking for him, eager to even up the score. But then, the answer came to her, and Mary fought against the urge to vomit all over Junior.

The doorbell... Grandma Miller. That's whose blood Junior was wearing now like a fifty dollar suit. She swallowed the feeling and hoped it stay buried. "Listen, dear... sir, I've been thinking."

"Have you? Maybe you should leave the thinking to me. It didn't work out so good for you last time, now did it?"

I want to scratch your eyes out and stomp on them.

"Well, it's silly, because I'm sure you've thought of it. Never mind." As Mary crossed back to the kitchen, she felt his eyes boring holes into the back of her head. Junior's gaze was among the most unpleasant things in the world, right up there with going to the dentist.

"Hey. Hold up," Junior began. "Thought of what?"

"It's nothing, like I said, sir. Nothing for you to get all worked up about."

He followed her into the kitchen. Mary hated when Junior trailed on her heels. She liked keeping an eye on him at all times, and without eyes in the back of her head, sometimes it was near impossible. Like now, when she was playing a different game with him. Matching wits, which put her at a tremendous advantage since Junior was short in the wit department. She was the cat, and he was her little mousy.

Mary sat at the table, a fresh river of sweat dripping down her thighs. She lit a cigarette and coughed an exhale. *Maybe Mrs. Garriga heard something. Saw something. Surely someone saw Grandma Miller arrive. Right?*

Junior smirked. "When did you start smoking?"

"Careful, sir. Curiosity killed the cat." She blew a misshapen smoke ring at his face.

Junior sucked it in as though he were sniffing a bouquet of

fresh wildflowers. "Killed the dog, too."

Mary winced, shouldering an imaginary blow right to her gut. *Poor, poor Justin.* "Have you thought about how we're going to cook dinner, dear?"

Junior pointed to the stove with an expression that said *duh, obviously.*

"Right. If only I'd thought of that." Mary took a quick drag on the cigarette. "Have you tried using the gas since the power went out?"

"What's the electricity got to do with the gas?"

"Nothing." Junior appeared dumbfounded. "Except they're provided by the same company. On the same bill. A bill I'm guessing hasn't been paid in some time."

"Huh. You mean?"

Mary nodded slowly at him, encouraging his use of his gray cells. "We've been shut off."

"No shit?" He walked over to the stove and flicked on a burner. It made a loud *click, click, click* sound, but there was no blue flame to ignite the burner. "Huh. Would you just look at that shit."

Mary sighed. *You can't lead a horse to water.* "So, we're going to need to cook the old-fashioned way, unless you're going to pay the bill."

"I can grill the meat in the yard."

"It's still cold, right? We can't eat it if it spoils. We'll get sick. You got enough ice?"

"Yes, I got enough ice, little miss smarty-fucking-pants."

"It's really hot in here, is all I'm saying. Ice melts. The meat won't stay fresh for long once it thaws."

"Then I'll get more ice." Junior shrugged. "Frozen water is cheap enough. Cheaper than paying the gas man."

"Do you need help bringing the grill up from the basement?" Their father hadn't used the charcoal grill in at least two summers. He wasn't very good at grilling, and they all liked to rib him about it. The poor guy eventually got so tired of hearing how inedible his burgers were that he tossed the grill in the basement next to the seven-foot plastic Christmas tree. *Go big, or go home*, Billy Sr. had said in the Sav-Mart when he spotted the tacky white plastic tree.

"No," Junior stammered. "I'll get it myself. Besides, grilling is men's work. You should get to tidying up this place. It's looking like a real sty."

Sooooo-iieeeee. Pig, pig, pig.

"Sure. I'll get right on that, dear." Mary stubbed out the cigarette.

Oink, oink.

He leaned in and kissed her gently on the forehead. "You know I love you, right, Mary?"

Mary? She stared at him, frozen in place. Junior hadn't even realized what he'd said, that he'd slipped and broken character. *Oh no, what do I do? I can call him out on it, and this can finally be—*

No, the voice said clearly. *Not yet.*

"Yes, sir."

Junior sauntered off toward the basement door. He held a shiny silver key in his hand.

"Hey, I wanted to ask you something," she called to him.

Junior stood still and circled his head back to meet her eye. "Yeah? What was that? The suspense is killing me."

"The note."

"Uh-huh. What about it? I'm not getting any younger here, Mare."

158

Mare. That was his nickname for her. Her pet name.

"Could you... read it to me?"

Junior sighed. "Again?"

"Again," she said with a small nod. "Yes, please. Again."

"I don't know why you gotta hear it again, but sure. Okay. Anything for my Mary."

Mary. He said it again. What is up with him today? He is acting odd. Different, for sure, even for Junior. Very out of character.

It was almost as though something had finally snapped in him.

He rifled through his pockets and finally pulled a folded sheet of white paper out of their depths. Mary stood and took a few cautious steps toward him as he unfolded the wrinkled paper and read, "Dear kids. Your mom and I have to go away for a few days to take care of something urgent for Grandma Miller. We'll be back before you know it. We're leaving Junior in charge. Do what he says without question. We've devised a game we think you'll enjoy and will help pass the time. See you soon. Love, Mom and Dad."

Mary flicked her tongue over her chapped lips. Something wasn't right.

Junior shrugged. "That's all she wrote. They wrote, I guess." He folded the note in half.

"Read it again, sir."

"Again?"

"Yes, please. Again." And now she thought she knew what it was; the thing he'd done, the thing that nagged at her.

"Why should I read it again? Wasn't you listening the first time, you useless skinbag?" Junior sounded annoyed now.

"I thought you said you'd do anything for me, sir." Her eyes studied his reaction.

Junior's eyes looked away from hers, and he recoiled. That was when she knew—the moment Junior flinched.

He smiled at her, but it was not the loving smile of a dutiful husband fulfilling his wife's wish or even the placating smile of a brother. No, Mary thought Junior's smile was a nervous one. He looked like the kid in class the teacher called on because they knew he wasn't listening. Junior's smile read something like *hoping for the best.* "All right." Another weak smile. "Anything for you, Mare."

Mary stepped closer to him. Junior's hands fumbled awkwardly with the paper. "Dearest kids. We had to go away for a few days to take care of something important for Grandma Miller. We'll be back real soon. We're leaving Junior in charge. Do what he says without any questions. We thought of a game we think you'll like to pass the time. See you soon. With love, Mom and Dad." He folded up the paper and buried it deep inside his front pocket.

But Mary had seen it for herself, had heard it even. Now, something she'd been wondering about since the game began suddenly became clear and presented her with more questions.

There was no note from their parents. She'd seen through the paper the second time Junior "read" it, and the page was blank. It was nothing but a crinkled, folded piece of notepaper. Junior couldn't even remember what it was supposed to say, what their parents supposedly had left behind before leaving them in Junior's care.

Mary wasn't a stupid girl. Naïve, perhaps. Inexperienced, definitely. But Mary Miller was, by any measure, an intelligent and thoughtful young woman. And her ability to detect bullshit grew stronger every day. She trusted her maturing instincts, and one thing Mary Ilene Miller was now certain of was that this was all a lie. Everything. That first nagging thought she'd had when he suggested the game had been correct.

It was all about *her*.

What's That I Smell Cooking?

Dinner had been, thankfully, uneventful. Everyone was too hot and tired to talk, so they ate in silence. Mary had to admit Junior did a fine job grilling the meat. Her belly rumbled when the first tantalizing whiff of the sizzling meat wafted through the back door, smelling positively divine, like food from the gods. It tasted even more heavenly. Tender. Juicy.

The bites melted in her mouth, but not before delivering a flavor bomb to the tongue. The taste was unique. Mary couldn't place it. Familiar, but also unfamiliar. Not unlike chicken, but not really like it. And it didn't quite taste like beef, either. When she'd finally asked him what exactly they were eating, Junior said the meat was a mix of pork and venison. And its one-of-a-kind flavor came from a blend of special secret spices and seasonings the butcher used.

Mary's bullshit alarm went off. She wondered first how Junior had paid for the meat. And then, when had he gone out to buy it? But her doubts didn't stop her from downing two platefuls. She didn't care if it was skunk, cat, or dog. All she cared about was that there was still something to eat.

Mary couldn't think on an empty stomach. She *needed* to eat. And until her metabolism slowed the fuck down, she was going to stuff her face as often as she could. Mary might get a little buzz from a sip of wine at church on Easter Sunday, but she could eat Junior under the table.

Old Mr. Pastori, the host at Patrizio's Eatery, always dreaded seeing the Millers walk through the door for the all-you-can-eat brunch buffet. *Slow down, girl! Breathe! Someday you gonna choke like that fatty rock star who died stuffing her face with a ham sandwich.* Old Mr. Pastori was, of course, talking about Mama Cass, who, contrary to urban legend, died of heart failure and not a piece of lunchmeat.

If there had been more of the meat, Mary would have devoured it in one gigantic gulp and gone back to lick the plate clean. But for now, there was no more. They'd eaten every morsel Junior grilled, with Mary eating the largest portion. It would have to do. Even though she was already counting down the hours until their next meal, now that her belly was full and somewhat satiated, Mary Miller could finally think.

Just Say a Little Prayer

Before falling into bed, Mary checked on Alex and Toby. They appeared listless all day from the heat building up in the house. Junior refused to let in any air from outside. He felt it would only make the house even hotter, letting in more moisture on top of the heat. *Besides,* he'd said. *If we open a window, all the cold air trapped inside will just fly out the window.*

Mary knew whatever cold air had been chilling around the house was long gone. She had to surgically peel off the clothes from her skin, with precision and dexterity. Mary swapped her clothing three times that day—four times if you count one additional panty swap because her undies had been soaked with sweat. By the end of the day, Mary and the kids lounged around the sweltering house in nothing more than bathing suits. Mary had chosen the most conservative of her bathing suits. Junior had already seen more than enough of her skin, and she had no desire to willingly parade any more of it in front of his eager eyes.

The kids took long, cold baths after supper, but the relief was temporary. Their faces flushed almost immediately after getting out of the tub, and Toby's breathing sounded more labored than usual. Hot and humid New York summers exacerbated his underlying allergy and asthma issues. Their parents sometimes sent him to Vegas during August when New York City was ripe and cooking, because while Vegas could roast at one hundred and ten degrees by noon, it was a dry heat. And that was infinitely easier on Toby's lungs. He didn't feel like he was drowning every time he tried to breathe. Plus, he could enjoy the outdoors.

Grandma Miller had a pool surrounded by lush palm trees, and the leaves kept her yard bathed in shadows when the sun was at its highest point in the sky. He still couldn't overdo it, but at least he wasn't trapped inside, staring at the television or playing video games all day. In Vegas, Toby could be a real boy and explore that curious side of him that always fell dormant over the summer at home.

Summers are for adventures and stories, and you'll find neither parked on the couch, young man, Grandma Miller once said. If she could just see them now.

"Here, take these. Quickly," Mary said, dropping two Midols in Alex's upturned palm. "It'll help with the pain. And the bloating."

Alex said nothing, just gave a small nod. She popped the pills in her mouth and swallowed them dry with ease.

"How *do* you do that?" Mary laughed.

"Years and years of practice." Alex beamed. Swallowing pills was a life skill she'd picked up thanks to years of persistent headaches and sinus infections. By the time she was six, she could gulp half a dozen adult-sized vitamins at once without a single drop of water. Alex never told her parents, or Mary, that while preparing to astonish and amaze the family with that feat of prestidigitation, she'd nearly choked to death on a chalky vitamin C tablet. That was a secret she'd take to her grave. One of them, anyway.

Mary gave her a light peck on the forehead and turned to leave when Alex called out, "Mar—I mean, Mom."

Mary mouthed, "Be careful" and then said aloud, "What is it, dear?"

"The bad man won't come anymore, right? Because I'm... not well?"

"What do you mean not well? Are you talking about your period?"

Alex nodded. She turned her face, a shameful look washing over it.

"You're not sick, kiddo. It's normal. Every girl gets her period at some point."

"But..."

"What?"

"It hurts."

Mary stepped back into the room and sat on the edge of the bed. Gently, she stroked Alex's face. "I know. The first one is the worst. But tomorrow it'll feel a little better, and the pills should help. I'll give you two more tomorrow just..." Her voice cut off. Then she continued in a whisper, "Don't let him see, okay?"

Alex nodded. "Because I'm a boy."

"Exactly. Because, for now, you're a boy."

"And he'll be mad if he sees I'm a girl."

"Yes." *God, yes.* "Yes, he will be. So we can't let him find out. We can't let him see you bleeding, okay?"

Alex gave her an unconvincing nod. "Mar—Mommy, I don't like this game anymore. When is Mom, *real* Mom, coming back?"

I don't like it either, kiddo. "I don't know, sweetheart. Soon, I think. Maybe tomorrow. We'll just have to see, won't we?

It'll be like waking up on Christmas morning. Maybe we'll run down the stairs and she'll be sitting in the kitchen, sipping her coffee and doing the crossword."

"That's what I'm gonna pray for tonight."

"Me too," Mary said with a smile. *Me too, kiddo. Me too.* "Now, go to sleep, young *man.*"

"Yes, Mommy." Alex winked at her as Mary slid through the door and tapped it closed gently behind her. She stood at the door and listened as Alex prayed softly. "Now I lay me down to sleep. I pray the Lord my soul to keep. Should I die before I wake, please, dear Lord, my soul to take. Please bless Mommy, my real Mommy, and Daddy, too. And Mary, Toby, and Justin. You can skip Junior. Please bring Mommy and Daddy home." And then she was silent. Mary was about to walk across the hall to check on Toby when Alex suddenly said in a voice so quiet Mary had to press her ear against the door to hear it. "And please keep the bad man away tonight. It hurts."

Doing the Unthinkable

Toby was fast asleep, his breathing slow but not strained. By all outward accounts, the boy seemed to sleep restfully and comfortably despite the oppressive heat. There was even a hint of a smile on his face. Whatever he was dreaming, Mary hoped it was a good one.

Her dreams lately tended to be nightmares. Even the ones where she escaped the house with the kids and Justin—*poor, poor Justin*—were riddled with violence. And blood. Lots of blood. Last night, she'd dreamt she stabbed Junior while he was still asleep in bed. Staked him with a piece of the banister like Dracula in the grave. Junior woke, screaming. His blood painted Mary's face red and splattered the ceiling and walls. The white bedspread was covered in his blood by the time he uttered one final, bitter gasp—

—*you stupid cunt*—

—and then he burst into flames and was no more. Mary scooped up the kids and ran into the bright light of the sun with Justin, where their parents and Grandma Miller waited with open arms. Her mother's arms felt so secure wrapped around her. She'd almost forgotten what it felt like to be safe, to feel loved. When she woke up and saw Junior fast asleep beside her, Mary covered her face with a pillow to muffle the sobs.

The thought of covering *his* face with the pillow didn't occur to her.

Besides, she was waiting for it—the voice—to tell her it was time to do the unthinkable.

Endings Are Hard

Mary shook the puffer at her ear. The canister held little medicine to begin, and now it sounded damn near empty. They'd be lucky to stave off another asthma attack. She wondered if she could somehow call Doc Gohlinghorst for a refill. But how would she pick it up? Junior wouldn't let her stroll out of the house to walk to the pharmacy. That would be a trap, and she knew it.

In the game, Alex was the one who should have asthma and not Toby. Their roles were reversed, as were their conditions. Mary didn't think that through at first. A part of her never dreamed this stupid game would go on this long. She thought their parents would be gone for the weekend and that would be that. As the days stretched into weeks, Mary wondered if they were ever coming back. Unless, of course, they *couldn't.* And ever since this afternoon, when she'd known for certain there was no note from their parents, Mary wondered what else Junior was keeping from her. Did he know where they were? Where they *really* were? Worse, was he the reason they were gone in the first place?

Somehow she'd have to get Toby a fresh puffer. Another day or two in this heat and he was doomed for another fit of asthma. And if push came to shove, Junior would let Toby die before ending the game. They were past the point of no return. The end was in sight, just around the bend, but she couldn't see it yet. But she knew the only way she was going to walk out of that house was over Junior's dead body.

Please, just say the word.

But the voice was silent.

Mary had enough of the voice's bullshit. All she had to decide was when she'd act without the voice's consent. *This has gone on for too long. It needs to end. Somehow... it needs to end.*

Salvation Lay Within

Junior was asleep by the time Mary crawled into bed around twelve thirty. She was surprised he was cocooned under the comforter, when even in her bathing suit, she was drenched in sweat. But Junior looked cool as ice, with just a sliver of his face poking out of the heavy blanket. Not a single drop of sweat Mary could see. It annoyed her that he seemed so comfortable when she was a slick mess of sweat and stink.

She lay on top of the covers cautiously, but Junior stirred in his sleep anyway. He tossed and turned for a moment and then settled back into what Mary thought was a deep sleep. Lying beside him, she could see more of his face entombed by the fluffy quilt. She'd forgotten how angelic Junior looked. His face had a youthful innocence about it, cherub-esque—like he'd stepped out of a Renaissance painting—but it was rarely visible in recent years. The deceptive face of the devil.

They were never close, even as children, despite the narrow gap of two years between them. But it felt like two lifetimes to Mary. They couldn't have been more different. Mary sometimes wondered if she wasn't adopted because she was so unlike her siblings. Of the four, Mary was most similar to Justin. They were both highly intelligent but quiet individuals who were loyal, sometimes to a fault. And if they possessed a fatal flaw, it would be their lack of gall. They were passive, or as Junior so often chided, *followers, not leaders.* They had no "balls," which, in Mary's case, was quite true.

Junior was always quick to remind them he was a leader. People did whatever he wanted. He was a *natural.* Even when the answer was no, as it so often was, Junior somehow found a way of turning a definitive "no" to a shaky "maybe" and then to a resounding "yes." It had been that way with the reissued Dakotah Dark albums. Their mom had been adamant that she didn't want any of the "devil's music" in their house, but by the end of the week, Junior was blasting Dakotah Dark through headphones twenty-four seven.

Grandma Miller once called Junior oily, like a used-car salesman minus the silver tongue. She did little to hide her disdain for Junior, nor he for her. They were oil and water, and Junior was the only one excused from spending time with Grandma Miller when she jetted into town for the holidays.

Junior could fend for himself for a couple of days if need be while the rest of the family traipsed across the country for a visit. The Garrigas would check on Junior and report back so their parents never regretted leaving him behind. Junior preferred it, and so did Grandma Miller.

Why was Junior covered in blood? And, more importantly, whose blood? Was that nagging in her stomach right, and was Junior covered in bits of Grandma Miller? If so, where was she? Did Junior stash her in the basement like Norman Bates stashed his dear old dead mommy?

Poor, poor Justin.

She had no reason to question Junior's story about a fight, but still, she did. It wasn't like he'd never gotten into a fight before, but this felt different to her. Maybe he had beaten some

173

stray dog.

Poor, poor Justin.

What or who had Junior gotten physical with? He didn't have so much as a single scratch under that blanket of blood, and she'd looked him over carefully after he'd showered. Junior was a decent fighter, but Mary couldn't see how he could come home drenched in blood without a single mark on him. Not even a bruise on his knuckles, the telltale sign he'd been in a fight. It nagged at her. Her mind picked at it like a scab. One minute he was in the house, and the next, he was outside. And when he returned, he was covered in blood.

It all started with that damned doorbell. Junior jumped up as though someone had lit an actual fire under his ass. He saw who was on the other side of the door. She hadn't. Junior had made sure of that, hadn't he? Whoever it was got Junior's panties twisted in a way she'd never seen before. That nosey Mrs. Garriga wouldn't have gotten a rise out of him. She'd been poking around the last few days anyway, but couldn't bring herself to step more than a few feet onto the driveway before tucking tail and going back under her rock. Or so Junior had told her. Had he lied about that too?

No, there was only one person on God's green earth that scared Junior enough for him to spring into action the way he had. And that was...

All I have to say is...

Grandma Miller.

... you'd better be dead when I get out there. Otherwise, I'll kill you.

Hope all is well.

No. It couldn't be. Could it?

See you in a day or so.

She *had* come after all. Come to save them from Junior.

And Junior had...

What? Killed her?

Ha, as if. Junior couldn't... wouldn't.

Or would he?

Sure, he and Grandma Miller didn't get along. They probably hated each other, but he wouldn't actually *kill* her.

Would he, though?

No.

But why?

And then it hit her. She held her breath as her heartbeat pounded, and every part of her froze in place. Mary lay beside her possibly murderous brother, paralyzed with fear and a growing sense of horror and dread.

The game. He didn't want her to end the game. That's why.

The voice spoke up, clear and deliberate. *You know he could.*

No, he couldn't.

You know he did.

No, he didn't.

And what about Fido? Justin?

He... he...

Ran off?

Yes, he ran off.

Then where is he, Mary? Why hasn't he come back with help?

Mary couldn't think. Her temples throbbed. A dull ache quickly spread through her head until it moved in behind her eyes.

Maybe you should see for yourself, Mary.

See what?

Not what, *Mary. Where.*

The voice tried her last nerve of patience. She wanted to scream at it but realized she was arguing with herself.

Fine. Where then?

You know where, Mary.

Where?

All roads lead to the basement, Mary.

What's in the basement?

You know.

I...

You know, Mary. You know. Follow the smell.

Mary didn't want to know any of it. She just wanted to lie there like a lifeless rag doll and die. That was one way to end the game, but she had Alex and Toby to think about. If Junior had... if he had done... *something* to Grandma Miller... and Justin, what would he do to the kids if she wasn't there to stop him?

Suddenly, a hand swept over the top of her sweat-soaked bathing suit and over her breast. She tried to move but couldn't. It was as though her limbs were made of lead. The image of Junior covered in blood, grinning with devilish delight, flickered in her mind. He continued to grope her, his hand alternating from one breast to the other. Out of the corner of her eye, she caught sight of him, face feverish and flushed. His breath was slow and heavy. Slowly, he pulled the blanket away from his body, and she realized then not only was Junior naked, but the awful thing between his legs was very awake. It pulsed and throbbed harder than she'd ever seen it before, and it repulsed her.

Junior's hands returned to her breasts, this time slipping under the fabric of her bathing suit to pinch her nipples. Gradually, his fingers moved around to her back and then up to her neck, where they found the tie that held up her suit. Before she knew what was happening, his fingers had easily undone the tie, and his hands were pulling off her bathing suit.

No. No. No.

She wanted to say this aloud, but the words wouldn't form. Her mouth remained firmly shut, lips glued together, as Junior tossed the suit on the floor and took in her naked form. Somewhere in that secret place deep within her mind, Mary screamed loudly as Junior mounted her and pushed apart her legs. They felt like jelly in his firm grip, lame and numb to the touch.

No. No. No.

With a loud, guttural groan, Junior pushed that thing inside of her until his hips met hers and then remained still with his awful thing buried deep inside her. Tears rolled down her cheeks, the only form of expression that hadn't failed her. After a moment, Junior sighed and groaned and moved his hips, thrusting in and out of her. The pain shot through every inch of her body like a bolt of lightning. Wetness grew between her legs, in her special place, but it didn't ease the pain. That she was bleeding, she knew without looking.

The air in the dark bedroom reeked of blood and sweat.

Junior grunted some more, thrusting himself into her harder and faster with growing determination. Her body shook under his weight. Her face soaked in the stray drops of sweat pouring down his face. Junior closed his eyes and scrunched his face, driving his pelvis at her with ferocity. He let out a loud moan and collapsed on top of her, his body twitching in a series of spasms as he grunted into her ear. The area between her legs felt soaked as blood and fluid, some hers and some undoubtedly his, oozed down her thighs.

Junior became dead weight on top of her, smothering her.

Mary couldn't breathe. It was as though there was no oxygen left in the room. Her chest rose and fell rapidly as sweat poured off every inch of her exposed flesh. Mary felt dirty and not just physically. It was wrong, so wrong what he'd done—what they'd done.

Oh god, there are words for this. Awful words for this. It's wrong. It's illegal. We're going to hell for this.

She cried harder without making a sound.

It didn't take long for her to realize Junior was asleep, still inside of her, but his awful thing was softening and slipping out of her wetness. His arms enveloped her and pulled her limp body to his, and he uttered three words in a gentle, warm voice.

"I love you."

A moment later, Junior snored in her ear, and he was out of her entirely.

I'm scared of the bad man, she remembered Alex saying.

Mary knew then that she could do it.

That she *would* do it.

She was already bound for hell, so it made little difference to her now to commit yet another sin. After all, nothing could be more terrible than what she'd just done. Nothing. And if there was a god up there, looking down on her, she knew it would understand. It might even sympathize with her just a little.

And if this god didn't do it, she would gladly do it herself.

Day Seventeen: Junior Miller Eats Shit

High-pitched, fevered screams startled Mary awake. She bolted upright and ran down the hall, leaving a slick trail of sweat behind her. The house felt hotter than usual after two days without air conditioning or ventilation. The house was basically an Easy-Bake Oven, and she was roasting in it.

Toby stood outside the door to Alex's bedroom, which was *his* bedroom, but belonged to Alex for the duration of the game. A steady flow of tears ran down his cheeks.

Mary rushed to him, doing her best to comfort the child. "What is it? What's wrong?"

Toby merely shook his head and then pointed into the bedroom. Mary turned her head frantically toward a blood-soaked bed, which was missing a child.

The bad man.

I'm scared of the bad man.

That was what Alex had said.

"Stay here."

"No, don't go in there, Mommy. Please, don't go in there." Toby cried harder. The words were barely audible between sniffles and sobs.

"You know I have to." Mary crouched down and squeezed his shoulders. "Stand right here. I'll be able to see you, and you can see me. Nothing is going to happen."

"To either of us?"

Mary laughed. "To either of us."

"Promise?"

She held up her right hand. "Promise."

Toby considered for a moment and then gave her a nod. "But only for a minute."

"But only for a minute," Mary repeated in a whisper.

She removed her hands from the boy and rose to her feet. For a second, everything looked fuzzy, and Mary suddenly felt lightheaded, her legs turning wobbly. She steadied herself, placing a hand on the doorframe. Between the extreme heat and her empty stomach, it was no wonder she felt unsteady. Mary took a few deep breaths—in through the nose and long exhales out through her mouth. Soon, her vision cleared and feeling returned to her lower extremities. She took another deep breath and approached the small bed.

Oh, my god.

The covers were pulled back, and the pillows were thrown about. A corner of the sheet had come undone, revealing the mattress beneath, and right in the center lay a large circular blood spot. On the floor beside the bed lay a ripped pair of cotton panties.

Bad man.

Those two words kept repeating in her head. And then, *I'm scared of.*

"He came for her," Toby said in a soft voice laced with fear.

"Who did?" she asked, but she knew already what the boy would say.

"The bad man."

Mary didn't want it to be true, but she knew it was. She kept her back to Toby just long enough so he wouldn't see her cry.

She cried because Mary knew Alex was gone, and she would never, ever see her again.

Getting Busy

Joanne Garriga was the neighborhood busybody. Everybody knew it. Even she knew it. She wore it like a badge of honor. "I'm just looking out for my friends and neighbors," she'd say in her own defense. "Somebody has to. Someday, you'll thank me." And as Joanne Garriga raised the binoculars to her eyes to once again study the unsettlingly still and deeply dark Miller house through the slats in her bedroom blackout blinds, Joanne wasn't sure if "someday" hadn't finally arrived wearing a big old fucking bow.

It was the noises that made her stomach turn over the most. And then, strange enough, the lack of noise. One minute it sounded like something, or was it someone, was clawing at the basement walls, and then the house fell quiet as a grave.

Disembodied moans. Groans. Cries in the night. It was all right out of *Dark Shadows, she thought.* If that house wasn't haunted, Joanne Garriga would turn in her busy-body badge to the main office, wherever the hell that was.

Last night, something putrid piggybacked on the evening breeze into her window and traveled straight up her nostrils. It was a sick smell, like something she caught wind of once when her mother lay still in her final hours in hospice.

That was what had really gotten to her. The smell. More than

Junior skulking around at odd hours with a strange mustache drawn on his face. More than the noises, the disembodied groans, and creaks that seemed to come from every bone in the Miller house itself.

She thought Cassie Miller would put an end to whatever shenanigans were going over there. That woman meant business, and she scared Joanne shitless. It was like she was ten years old talking to the nuns at St. Christopher's all over again. But even Catholic school nuns had nothing on Cassie Miller.

Joanne was sure she'd seen Cassie Miller arrive. She'd recognize that woman's gait anywhere. Determined, precise. Old as she was, Cassie Miller moved with purpose in every step. Joanne thought she'd seen Cassie go to the front door, then round to the side and back of the house.

But what then? Had she gone in? Broken a window and crawled right on in?

No, she wouldn't do that. Not when she could've gone into the death house through the cellar door. That's what she did. Joanne was sure of it. Only, she never saw Cassie Miller come out of the house.

Could she still be there, inside somewhere, Joanne wondered. Why hadn't she come out?

The not knowing what was going on was eating at her. It was worse than an itch that couldn't be scratched, and she knew it. Lately that damned house was all she could think about day and night. The damned Miller house, and the secrets that lay under its roof and inside its walls.

Tomorrow, Joanne thought, she'd have another little pow-wow with good old Bob Buchanan. One way or another, she'd get to the bottom of things.

"Joanne," her husband barked from downstairs. "Would you put them spy glasses down, and leave those people alone? How would you like it if someone was running surveillance on you?"

Yes, Joanne thought as she lowered the binocs.

Somehow, someway, she'd get that house to spill its guts. Even if she had to kill Bob to do it.

"Because someday you'll thank me. You'll ALL finally thank me," she said to the Miller house, knowing it was listening. A big, hopeful smile took shape on her otherwise expressionless face.

It's a Sin

"Eat it. You know you want to," Junior said, waving a plateful of meat under her nose.

"I said I'm not hungry." This was a lie. She was *starving*, and the meat smelled better than usual. But a sick feeling gestated in her barren belly, a feeling not even Junior's mystery meat could abate.

"Come on now, girl. You know you need to eat. This here is hard to come by. We can't just let it go to waste now, can we?"

True, there wasn't much food to come by, and there was no telling when the supply of meat would dry up. Any meal could be their last. Only Junior knew how much meat remained, and he wasn't sharing that information.

Her stomach grumbled loudly. "Fine."

Junior laughed as she grabbed the paper plate.

"But only because it's a sin to waste perfectly good food."

"Oh, my little darling. Don'tcha know, some of the best things in life are a sin." Junior winked at her.

It had been a sin, what they'd done in bed, and it was also illegal. She knew that. Junior didn't care, but she did. If she was sorry and if she prayed hard enough, the Almighty would forgive her. After all, hadn't Mary Magdalene herself once been a whore? Who knows? Maybe she was Christ's whore. If the Lord could stand to be around such a woman and let her wash his feet, surely such a divine intelligence could forgive her for doing what she had to do to survive. It was the good old Catholic get-out-of-hell-free card—just say you're sorry, and all is forgiven. Only, Mary didn't know if she was truly, heartfully sorry, and He'd know if she was telling a lie. For now, she didn't say the words, only ruminated on them and saved her free pass for another sin.

Mary devoured the meat without stopping for air. She could almost think straight again, but that portion nowhere near satiated her agonizing hunger. More. She wanted—*needed*—more. And there should be more, she suddenly realized. They were one Miller short, after all.

"He's gone, you know." She'd almost slipped and called Alex a "she." It was getting harder to keep it all straight in her head. She was losing the thread back to reality. "There was blood," Mary said matter-of-factly. She knew Junior was already aware of her absence since he was the one who sent her away.

"Yeah, well, you know how it is sometimes. Kids... they bleed."

"Some of them. Sometimes."

Junior nodded. "Girls, like you, bleed. Little boys don't bleed unless you make them bleed."

"What did you do, dear?" The word "dear" hung between them until Mary cleared it. "Sir."

"Rules is rules, dear. He broke the rules, and he had to be punished. That's the game, ain't it?"

"Yes, dear." *Ask him about the meat.*

"Daddy knows best, right?" Junior lit a cigarette and took a long, slow drag.

186

"Yes, dear." *God, that smells good. I want a smoke. Ask him about the meat.*

"Will he be coming back?"

"No." He blew smoke through his nose like a dragon. "I wouldn't expect him to come back."

"I see." *Ask him.* "Can I have his portion of the meat?"

Junior's eyes lit up. He smiled and slid a paper plate across the table to her. It was a smaller helping, a child's portion. Mary buried her face in it and ingested the small pile of mystery meat without ever taking a single bite. When she'd finished, she let out a raucous, sulfuric burp.

"That's my girl," Junior said with an approving smile.

Masks

Toby kept to himself for the rest of the day, hiding out in Alex's bedroom—his for the game. Normally, Toby enjoyed spending time in Alex's room, but not so much today. There was no Alex, and that was a loss Toby felt deeply.

They were less than a year apart and so alike that their mom used to say she'd been blessed with twins without having to carry them both at the same time. And that was how they thought of each other. Not just as mere siblings, but twins. Their bond went deeper than blood. They shared part of the same soul.

Sometimes, their bond creeped out the rest of the Millers. They *knew* things about each other, things that were never said aloud, things that didn't *need* to be said aloud. During long car rides, not that there had been many, Alex and Toby would simultaneously break into a fit of hysterical laughter as though they had heard the same punchline, but no one had said a single word aloud.

In first grade, Toby lost his favorite toy, Spot the dog. He came home screaming and fussing about how he'd killed Spot and what a terrible dog owner he was to have misplaced him. Alex slipped out of the room and returned a few minutes later with Spot. She'd *seen* exactly where Toby had left the thing.

She saw it in her mind, through *his* eyes.

Their connection went far beyond finding misplaced objects. Alex was afraid of needles. The first time she got a booster shot for school, she'd passed out cold. And forget drawing blood. That was a nightmare. But then, one day, the fussing stopped. She'd sat perfectly still as they poked and prodded her, smiling and giggling the entire time.

On the drive home, their mom had asked her what was so funny back there at the doctor's office; what had made her laugh so?

Alex had giggled again and said, without missing a beat, "Toby was telling me the funniest story."

For the briefest of moments, Alex thought she saw her mom's face turn to utter horror and panic, before it eased back into its normal mask.

There's Children in That There Corn, Ma

Denise Miller felt like someone had walked over her grave when her daughter said this. Toby hadn't been with them at the doctor's office. And Alex, whether she knew it or not, was talking about telepathy.

"This is too weird. We're talking about fucking Stephen King *Carrie* territory," Denise told Billy later that evening.

Billy wasn't nearly as concerned about Alex and Toby's connection. "Carrie White had telekinesis, not telepathy. She could move things with her mind. Come on, now. You can't possibly think they're actually talking to each other with their minds?"

She had, and the thought terrified her. Not because they shared something unique between them that no one else could experience, but because if Toby and Alex could do *that*, what *else* could they do?

Denise Miller watched her youngest kids like a hawk for months. There were things she couldn't explain. One morning she had spent ten minutes looking for her car keys, and then they randomly appeared on the kitchen table. Denise was positive she'd looked there, too. *Several* times. She would have bet her life on it. The whole time she was running through the house like a chicken without its head, Toby and Alex were sitting on the living room floor, lost in their own little world, giggling at a shared private joke. Denise knew *she* was that joke, but she couldn't prove it. And the more she talked about it with Billy, the crazier the whole idea sounded. *My kids blessed with special wonder-twin powers? Yeah... hardy-har-har. That's a good one.*

Still, the feeling never quite went away, but Denise tried not to think about it. She forced herself *not* to think about it, no matter what crazy shit she saw out of the corner of her eye. She'd just smile and say, *There's nothing to see here. Nothing at all.*

Toby knew all about the bad man and what he'd been doing to Alex. He didn't understand it at first. The images he saw in his head were confusing, too adult for his comprehension. But he understood the feelings perfectly.

Fear, pain, shame, and rage.

After the first couple of times, Toby slipped into her head and told her stories to keep her distracted until the bad man had finished. While he couldn't take away the physical pain after the bad man's visits, Toby shielded his sister from a great deal of psychological trauma.

Distracting her with his stories meant Toby saw everything, like he sucked a mouthful of snake venom out of her and poisoned himself. But Alex seemed mostly unaware of the rapes after a while. She stopped talking about the bad man's nocturnal visits with him entirely, but the images lived inside his head. And now that she was gone, Toby wasn't sure what to do with the rage brewing within his split soul.

He had wanted to do more to help his sister, his non-romantic soul mate, but he didn't think he could do it without her. Whatever they had shared, it only worked when they were together. Toby never could have hidden their mom's keys on his own. Neither could Alex. Their power, or whatever it was, just didn't work without the both of them. Alex told Toby that they were like batteries. One was positive and one was negative, and you needed both ends to power up their ability.

Toby closed his eyes and lay down on the bed. Even though he'd been sleeping in her bed for over two weeks, her scent lingered on the sheets. He conjured her in his mind, fleshed out every detail until he believed Alex *was* lying in bed beside him, stroking his hair soothingly. *It's okay, little brother. It's okay.*

But it wasn't. He was alone now, and he would always be alone from now on. A part of him was missing, and until they were together again, he'd be no more than a broken half. He thought of Junior sneaking into her room at night, pulling aside her panties and putting himself inside her, then slinking off into the darkness when he'd finished. Toby hated Junior for what he'd done to Alex, and then for taking her away from him.

Toby opened his third eye and extended an invisible hand through his mind. At first, his fingers fumbled through the dark, feeling nothing. Similarly, the eye saw nothing but black, as though it had been blindfolded. Some sounds and smells came from outside the house and some from within, but Toby couldn't see a thing.

His real fingers dug down and clutched the bedspread. The veins in Toby's arms popped as he squeezed the fabric into his fists. His sweat-soaked body thrashed furiously, and his slender legs kicked high into the air like a Radio City Rockette. Then every part of him tensed as Toby squeezed harder and deeper with his mind. He kept trying to find Junior, to *see* him. Toby's heartbeat accelerated and then halted.

A deep freeze tore through his body. He convulsed once, his body rising two inches off the mattress, then twice, and then a third time before it sank back down onto the bed where it remained still, cold, and nearly lifeless. Suddenly, he gasped and clamped down his jaws so ferociously that his mouth instantly filled with blood. His eye had opened.

Toby sought Junior in his head. He fixed on Junior like a beacon, concentrating on his brother until an image slowly formed. Fuzzy at first, but soon he could make everything out with perfect clarity. He had done it on his own, after all.

Junior sat at the kitchen table. He was sweating, smoking a cigarette that was nearly burnt to the butt, and pouring himself a beer. Toby went deeper into his mind, feeling the ability surge through him—a marvelous, blindingly bright light. Yet as bright as it shone now, it had burned even brighter when he was with Alex. Together, their blaze rivaled the sun.

He heard the steady rhythmic beat of Junior's heart and then a slow exhale of air and smoke through his mouth. A sip of cheap room temperature beer. Another long drag on the cigarette, which was now finished. Junior dropped the cigarette stub into the can where it sizzled and hissed before dying.

In his mindscape, Toby cracked one of the back legs of Junior's chair. The wood splintered as though it had been nothing but a twig. The chair wobbled, and a second later, Toby heard a loud crashing thud followed by a slew of profanity.

And he knew he'd done it. He'd really done it. Now the question was, what else could he do?

Alex giggled and sang inside Toby's racing thoughts. *Humpty Dumpty sat on a wall. Humpty Dumpty had a great fall...*

The twins conversed silently, speaking rapidly in the safety of their secret place.

Alex, you're here!

I am.

But where are you?

I don't know exactly. Close, I think. I can't really see.

Are you...

I don't know. Maybe.

How long can you stay?

Forever.

Toby laughed so hard he cried. The sound brought Mary to the door.

"Hey, kiddo. What's so funny?"

He rolled around on the bed as though being tickled by ten invisible fingers at once. "Nothing." Toby howled with laughter, holding his sides. "Alex just said something really funny."

"Well, keep it down. Daddy's in a mood." The Alex comment didn't register with Mary's own distracted mind.

Toby didn't keep it down. He laughed harder and harder until he couldn't breathe and damned near wet himself.

Mary went downstairs and found Junior still on his ass, covered in beer, cursing at everything in creation from Peter, Paul, and Mary to Jesus. She couldn't help but smile at him as he kicked the air and threw his hands up and down like a toddler.

Toby's laughing fit grew louder, and Mary laughed a bit herself. It was like hearing someone rip one out in church right in the middle of the sermon and trying not to cackle.

"What the fuck is so goddamned funny?" Junior said, trying to brush himself off from the tumble.

"Oh, nothing. Toby just told the funniest joke."

Alex might still be alive somewhere in the Miller house.

Somewhere close by. Junior hadn't killed her properly after all. She'd have to check. Junior kept secrets in the basement. Magazines. DVDs. Naughty stuff. She wondered what else he kept down there.

There was only one way to find out.

The Final Interlude

Even before Mr. Buchanan found the Millers' car parked behind the shopping plaza at the end of St. Augustine Place, about three and a half blocks away from their house, he had a bad feeling in his gut. It came with age and experience. The nosey neighbor, Mrs. Garriga, hadn't done much to lessen that feeling.

At forty-eight years old, he had both. It also came with the job. People laughed whenever he said that, like he was a private dick or something more "official" than a mere mail carrier for the postal service. But with twenty-four years on the job, Bob Buchanan had seen his fair share of freaky shit. Houses that fronted for brothels or crack dens. Hordes of migrant workers spilling out the back door of a house because a neighbor complained about "too many people" living next door. Homes overrun with cats or dogs—or both. Hoarders buried alive by mountains of debris. Adulterers indulging in a not-so-secret daytime tryst while a spouse was away at work. Neglected and abused kids. Abusive husbands. You name it, Bob Buchanan had probably seen it.

Walking through neighborhoods every day gave him eyes on household routines—laundry days, takeout days, preferred times for vacation. Bob Buchanan thought it was a lot like the old saying—rather elementary if you paid the slightest bit of attention.

That was the key. The only key. You had to pay attention.

For the new blood, this was next to impossible. They were the distracted generation—tech-obsessed, constantly tapping away at their cell phones or plugging their ears with headphones while the world twisted and turned around them. Bob Buchanan didn't own the latest gadgets and had no use for them. He still watched movies on VHS and the occasional DVD and listened to vintage vinyl and audio cassettes. He didn't know what an MP3 player was, nor did he care to find out. His cell phone, which he begrudgingly acquired in case of emergencies, was a decade-old flip phone Nokia that didn't even have a camera. The device did only two things—send and receive text messages and make emergency phone calls. For a whopping twenty-nine bucks a month, he still felt like he was grossly overpaying.

Fresh-faced mail carriers couldn't understand how or why Bob Buchanan could spend eight hours a day, walking around untethered to tech.

To stay sharp, Bob thought. After all, he never would have spied the voluptuous blonde on Elden who liked to shower with the window open every day at two fifteen if he'd been distracted by technology. *Just another perk of the job. Two perks, actually.*

Yes, there wasn't much Bob Buchanan hadn't seen in twenty-four years of delivering mail, except for maybe a serial killer. That was the holy grail of mail carrier stories. *That's nothing, Bill. I delivered mail to Son of Sam. Even talked to him once or twice.* Everybody liked a good serial killer yarn.

The feeling that something was terribly off had been nagging at him even before the hold mail request had been submitted.

197

And not long after, the Millers' car moved from their driveway. Bob Buchanan knew the Millers, knew them well and was on a first-name basis with the parents, Billy and Denise. He'd been their carrier when the youngest was born, and when Mary learned how to ride a bike. Hell, he saw Junior toss a football for the first time, too.

Bob Buchanan may have never stepped foot inside the Millers' house, but he knew them intimately, and he knew Billy was cheap. They'd never go on an actual vacation, other than their annual trip to see his mammy in Nevada, but that was always in March when the kids had spring break. Billy's idea of a vacation was staying home, drinking whatever beer was on sale at the supermarket and hanging out with the kids. He did it every year at the end of August.

This was unusual. *Most* unusual.

The Millers, like most of the families on his route, were creatures of habit. They rarely deviated from their routines. And if they did, it was unlikely to last more than a day or two and had an obvious explanation—the house needed painting, the car needed fixing, or they were waiting for the cable guy. In this case, it wasn't a mere one-off. It was going into its third week, and that was unusual. *Most* unusual.

Down at the post office, they joked that Bob Buchanan was nosy. He asked too many questions and got too involved in other people's business, specifically those on his route. And maybe that was part of it. Bob Buchanan was just a little bit too nosy for his own good. He couldn't help himself. Had he been in possession of Pandora's box, Bob Buchanan would have opened it to see inside. And that's exactly how he felt about the Millers' house. It was an itch that needed to be scratched until it bled right down to the bone.

Bob Buchanan spoke to Mrs. Garriga first. If anybody was a bigger busybody than him, it would be Mrs. Garriga. *I'm not just a member, Bob. Why, I'm the President of the whole damned busybody club.* Yes. Mrs. Joanne Garriga was all that, and more.

"No, no. I called Denise—when was this? Right after I spoke to you about the mail. I told her I'd hold the overflow and to give me a buzz when they're back."

"And has she called you?"

"Not yet. I mean, why would she? They're still on vacation, right?"

Unusual. Most unusual.

"Of course. Vacation." Bob Buchanan hadn't walked three steps before the busybody suspected something was up.

"Hey! They *are* on vacation, right?"

"What do you mean?"

"You don't think something happened to the Millers, do you, Bob?" From her tone, it was obvious that she thought something had happened to the Millers. Something bad.

"No," he said with a reassuring grin. "Not at all. I'm sure you'll be getting a postcard from Bora Bora soon enough."

The Millers' car was the sticking point. First, it sat in the driveway for days, and now it sat behind the plaza. Bob Buchanan could write off most of the unusual things he'd seen at the Millers over the last two weeks—and the wafting aromas seeping through the crevices of the house—but he couldn't explain the damned car. The Chevy was a jalopy, held together with tape and a prayer, but to Billy, it was a Tesla. He bragged about how he paid cash for it, but never said just how much. And because the vehicle was so old and had more miles under its belt than god, it cost next to nothing to insure. Regardless of what the thing was worth, Billy would never leave it unattended for days on end.

Never.

It was *unusual. Most* unusual.

It had been over twenty days since Bob Buchanan last saw any trace of the Millers when he walked up the front steps. He looked up, side-eyed, at the bedroom window at the Garriga house, where he knew Joanne would be watching him like a hawk, and rang the bell. She would be the lookout for whatever half-assed mission this turned out to be. Bob hoped Joanne Garriga's eyes were better than her discretion.

As with his last visit, Bob Buchanan didn't expect anyone to answer. Nor did he expect to hear anything inside the house. If it weren't for the car and his gut feeling, he'd believe the Miller family was indeed on vacation.

But Bob Buchanan knew better. He knew the Millers were holed up somewhere inside the house. And he would find them if it was the last thing he ever did.

Bob Buchanan was about to ring the fuck out of the bell when he stopped. He couldn't believe the awful, pungent odor. It hit him instantly and then surrounded him in a wall of stink. As the noxious cloud stung his eyes, tears rolled down his cheeks. Whatever was in his stomach gurgled loudly with a groan and a splat, then Bob Buchanan hurled his breakfast all over the Millers' front porch. The puddle of undigested bacon and eggs oozed down the landing, dripping down each step until it landed on the front walk.

Good, god. What is *that? What the hell is that stench?*

It was everywhere now, and there was no escaping it. He looked around, desperate to find someone else who smelled it, too. *Why hadn't the neighbors called anyone? Couldn't they smell it?*

Bob Buchanan covered his nose and mouth with a hand, but he could still smell *it.* The odor grew more familiar with every inhalation. He knew that smell—death and decay. As a boy, he'd been allowed a pet gerbil. One evening, he realized he hadn't seen the gerbil in a few days. The young lad poked his head into the cage, and the smell smacked his nose instantly, the very same aroma he inhaled now—only this was much, much worse. At the bottom of the cage, under a mountain of fluffy bedding, had been the rotting carcass of his beloved pet gerbil, neglected and dead for nearly a week. The boy, like the man, hurled chunks right into the cage, instantly burying the dead animal in a thick, mushy layer of vomit.

Instead of the buzzer this time, he tried the rusty doorknob. Bob Buchanan was surprised that it gave no resistance and turned easily. The door was unlocked. He stood with his hand wrapped around the knob, debating.

To open or not to open. That is the question.

He thought of the stories he could tell at the post office. Finally, after years of being the butt of everyone's jokes, they would listen. Enthralled, they would gobble up every word about the things he'd seen inside the Miller house. He'd have all the gory details firsthand, not that harpie, Joanne Garriga.

Who'd be President of the busybody club then? Bob smiled. Oh, to see the look on her face when she read...

The Legend of the Miller House on St. Augustine Place, as told by Bob Buchanan.

He felt feverish, almost light-headed, like Ralphie in *A Christmas Story* racing to decode the Little Orphan Annie's "secret" message. This was it. He knew it. The big one. The golden ticket at last.

He turned the knob fully to the right, and there was a *click.*

Bob held his breath as he pushed the door, but it stayed in place. *Warped wood,* he thought to himself. It was an old door, and it had been hotter than Hades and wetter than an otter's pocket for the last few days. He took a deep inhalation of the putrid air, and then a second later, Bob Buchanan shoved his shoulder against the front door with enough force to pop it open.

The house exhaled with great force, and immediately, a gust of the foulest smelling gas rushed at him. Bob threw up again, this time straight onto the floor, splattering a nearby chair. Slimy bits of food, spit, and bile covered the front of his uniform. He wiped at his shirt as though brushing away a family of flies, and misshapen chunks of food flew in every direction.

Trying to wave away the smell was pointless. The tangy scent of death hung like a thick blanket of fog hugging the road. And it was so hot inside the Miller house. Bob thought he was burning under a sunlamp. His hands dropped to his sides as though they were made of lead. He hadn't expected it to be easy, getting inside the house, but it was. So goddamned easy. When he retold it later, as he no doubt would with his ass parked on the last stool at O'Leary's on 51st Street, he'd have to say he broke in or found a hidden key somewhere. Something infinitely more interesting than walking leisurely through the front door as though he was expected for high tea.

As he made his way into the living room, Bob Buchanan realized it was no longer a home he'd stepped into, but a tomb. And the front door had been the lid on the sarcophagus.

Or was it plural—sarcophagi, Bob mused.

He closed the front door, and it made an awful sound as the warped wood screeched across the frame *Go back from whence yee came!*

Bob thought about his pet gerbil again as he stepped deeper into the tomb. He never felt more alive. His heart raced in his chest as a fresh and steady trail of sweat coated his sunburned face. His hands trembled, and both feet felt like they were made of jelly. This was exactly the way he felt all those years ago as he poked his head into that cage.

It was morbid, he knew, but there was something darkly exciting about death. Brushing up to it from a safe distance, knowing you could walk away with a whale of a tale. That was why those *Faces of Death* movies had been so popular before the internet came along with its all-access pass to the macabre, ruining all the fun of huddling around the television in someone's basement to watch a "forbidden" tape. People are fascinated by death. Why else do they slow down on the highway as they approach those flares signaling an accident ahead? Carnage. Oh, they pretend they're not going to look. Get all self-righteous. Shout at other drivers rubbernecking. But then, at the last possible moment, they do it anyway. We all do. We wait and wait and then turn our heads with ghoulish delight at the moment of opportune viewing, hoping to catch a glimpse of blood, viscera, a dislodged limb, or severed head rolling across the highway. And then we continue on our merry fucking way, sometimes with the social media post to end all posts:

So I was driving down 95, and you'll never guess what I saw in the middle of the road. <insert a hastily snapped photo of a severed head> Don't lose your heads, guys. It's almost the weekend. #drivesafe #yolo #truestory

This was different from his gerbil. Bob wasn't an idiot. He knew that. The Millers were people, not critters. And that made this even more exciting. It also made the scenario more dangerous. Maybe it was the fumes, the awful stench, or his own giddiness, but Bob didn't think for a moment anything bad would, or *could*, happen to him.

The Miller house was dark, especially now that the front door was closed.

Why did I shut it?

At first, all Bob could see were shapes jutting out in the darkness, which he assumed was the furniture he'd seen seconds ago. Gradually, his eyes adjusted, and the shapes filled with detail. The blinds were drawn on every window in the living room, as were the thick darkening drapes across the main front windows. Streams of sunlight snuck through tiny breaks in the blinds, but otherwise, the room was black.

Bob tapped the back pocket of his standard-issue U.S. Postal Service uniform shorts for his flip phone. It didn't have a flashlight setting, but he figured whatever light the screen provided was still better than wandering around in total darkness. The phone sprang to life with a low-tech musical fanfare. *Boo. Beep. Boo.* Bob covered the phone nervously, but it was too late. The phone's cheesy musical flourish had given his presence away. The sound had been low enough, but it seemed to echo through the still house.

He uncovered the phone and waved it through the air in front of him. The stairs leading to the second floor became visible, as did a door ahead in the living room. Bob waved the phone to his right. A corridor and then another room. The kitchen, he presumed. He'd start there, and then maybe give that door in the living room a go. *Basement,* he thought as he ambled toward the kitchen.

The smell grew weaker further away from the living room, but he noticed there an entirely different aroma in the kitchen.

The death smell was still present but layered under a more tantalizing one—the mouth-watering scent of seasoned meat. His stomach gurgled as he breathed in the delectable fragrance. He couldn't place it, but it didn't smell like chicken or pork. Bob Buchanan was a bacon connoisseur. He'd know the aroma of pig fat anywhere. Whatever it was, Bob felt no guilt hoping to find a leftover morsel of it somewhere in the house to sample for himself.

He passed the phone through the air. The kitchen, too, was dark. While the window above the sink had been covered with newspaper and magazines, bits of light streamed in through several curled pages. The first thing Bob noticed was the stillness. No ticking of a clock or hum of a refrigerator. Nothing but unsettling silence. A light switch jutted from the wall. He tried it several times, but no light came. The overhead lamp remained fast asleep.

Bob walked over to the fridge and opened the door. *My god.* He gasped loudly when he saw what was inside. He opened the drawers and checked the shelves on the door, but there was nothing. The fridge was completely bare. Dirty, its surface riddled with spills and streaks of various sauces and condiments, but devoid of any food. Then he noticed the garbage can in the corner overflowing with trash—plastic wrappers, soiled napkins, empty chip bags, paper plates. For a moment, he hoped there'd be a piece of that mystery meat left behind on a plate, but they looked licked clean—twice over.

Damn, he thought. He felt like a college kid all over again, desperate to lick the inside of a zip-lock plastic bag for any "magic" mushroom crumbs.

Bob was about to dig deeper into the trash when he heard a grunt, maybe a groan. It was faint but obvious. His mouth dried at the sound, and a nervous fart slipped past his clenched flabby middle-aged ass cheeks.

"Hello?" he said in a cracking voice far too soft for even a church mouse to hear. Bob grunted and cleared his throat, then tried again, this time with more force. "Hello?"

Nothing stirred, just more of the same eerie silence, but then he heard it again. So very faint, but it was there. It was the sound of someone in distress, someone below him... in the basement.

With the dim glow of his prehistoric cell phone to light the way, he moved through the kitchen and back into the living room with a speed and certainty that took him by surprise.

A hero. I can be a bloody hero.

When he reached what he presumed was the basement door, Bob was surprised to see it propped open just a sliver. He couldn't recall if the door had been ajar when he first entered the Miller house or not. The pungent odor of death was almost overpowering behind that door. *It's coming from down there.*

He reached for the knob but hesitated.

Maybe I should call for help first? That would be the... That would be a foolish thing to do. What do I do then? Sit on the porch like a lame duck until the cops arrive and let them take all the credit? This is my story, goddammit. All mine. MY golden ticket. MINE. Fuck it. I'm going in.

Bob pulled the door open. The smell soured his stomach, and he fought the urge to vomit once more. "Hello," he shouted into the darkness. "Is anyone down there? Are you hurt?"

A rattling sound, like that of a chain, followed by the clang of metal on metal.

And then Bob Buchanan heard it plain as day.

"Helllp meee."

"All right, I'm coming for you."

Bob all but ripped the door off the hinges, pulling it aside so he could rush to the rescue. His fingers had punched 911 on his device and now hovered on the bulky green dial button.

"I'm coming!"

"Help me. Oh, dear god... help meeeee! Please!"

Bob got one foot through the doorway when someone grabbed him from behind and threw him to the ground with ease. He landed on his back with a heavy thud. The phone slipped from his hand and slid across the room. The screen went dark.

"No, no, no!" a shrill voice screamed. "You can't be here! You're not supposed to be here!"

Bob lost his bearings. His breath was short, and his heart pounded rapidly in his chest.

"Please... help me," the voice from below bellowed again.

"You're not playing. You're not part of the game!" the voice shrieked.

Bob's blood ran cold. He knew that voice. But it sounded... different. *Crazed*. He must be mistaken. That was it. There was just no way on god's earth that voice belonged to—

The shape moved noisily through the darkened room. Before he could finish that thought, she was on him. The blade tore through his flesh with ease as she slammed it into his chest, burying it to the handle right through his heart.

"Mary," he said through a mouthful of blood.

And Mary, her eyes twisted and twitchy, laughed maniacally as everything went black. The story would die with Bob Buchanan.

The End of Days

On the morning of the eighteenth day of the game, Mary tried the phone again while Junior was out on another ice run. The runs to the store had gotten quicker. Mary didn't have a lot of time. She held the receiver to her ear and tapped at the hook switch several times, but the line was dead. Permanently dead. Their service had been cut off.

Maybe I can find the cell phones? One of them has to have a little juice in it.

Mary turned over the obvious places—couch, nightstand, under the bed—hoping to find a working cell phone or tablet. But she found nothing. She collapsed onto the mattress in a sweaty heap when lightning struck. Junior wasn't very imaginative with hiding Christmas or birthday gifts, and often, Mary knew weeks ahead of time what he had gotten for her. A shoebox at the back of the closet was his favorite hiding place for all kinds of stuff—sex mags, porno DVDs, and Dakotah Dark memorabilia.

She flung open the closet door and dove through the maze of hanging dresses and sports coats until she found herself sitting on the floor in the back of the closet where, hidden in plain sight, lay Junior's treasure trove. Mary's body shook with anticipation. She pried open the cardboard lid with her clammy

THE END OF DAYS

digits and peered inside the box.

Her heart sank instantly. It was like a graveyard. They were all broken beyond repair, destroyed by something like a hammer, she'd guess. Glass shards from shattered screens and electronic guts lined the inside of the box. Mary picked up each device and tried turning them on. If she could just get one, that was all she'd need.

Junior's phone emitted a long, loud beep and then fell silent, joining the other devices in premature death. *Murder.*

Come on. Come on, please! I just need to send a text to...
Grandma Miller.

Mary had forgotten all about her. Her memory... memories... were fuzzy. Why had Grandma Miller never arrived? The old woman had sounded determined in her messages, like she was going to get her old ass there come hell or high water.

The blood from earlier in the week still bothered her. She couldn't let it go. Just whose blood had Junior been bathed in three days ago? There was something there. She knew it, and she was on the trail like a bloodhound.

Suddenly, a sharp pain stabbed in her side. Hunger? She hadn't eaten any meat since last night, over twelve hours ago. Devouring her ration—as well as Alex's portion—hadn't filled her seemingly bottomless belly. Foraging for food would *have* to wait.

First, she had to get into the basement. *Come hell or high water...*

A Door Opens

Mary grabbed the butcher's knife from the kitchen and went to work on the basement door. It surprised her how fast she picked the lock. Her skills came rushing back as soon as she broke the paper clips in half to fashion the perfect lock-picking instruments.

As a kid, Junior had been really into magic. More escape artist type shit than "Nothing up my sleeve" or "Pick a card, any card" type of illusions. Houdini had been Junior's idol—until Junior cuffed himself to the train tracks and couldn't get out. The incident forced him to admit that he was no Houdini, and he promptly hung up his cuffs for good. But he had shown Mary a thing or two about picking everyday locks before replacing his Harry Houdini poster with Dakotah Dark.

Two quick jabs with the paper clip and the lock turned. As the tumbler slid and the lock clicked open, Mary laughed at what a good student she had been. Lock-picking might not show on her high school transcript, but Mary felt awfully proud for doing so well under pressure. She'd have to remember to pat herself on the back later when it was all over. And somehow, she sensed it would be—the game—all over soon enough.

The basement door popped open, and the stench hit her at once. Mary had never smelled anything so foul before. Not even the McCarthy Farms in Lawrenceville smelled this bad, and they had mounds of cow and pig shit everywhere. She gagged, covering her mouth, then froze where she stood.

"Helllp meee."

She barely made out the voice over the sound of her beating heart in her ears.

"Oh, god. Please help me. Please."

Then Mary heard the rattling of metal on metal and a chain dragging across the floor.

"Help me, please."

"Hello," she shouted down from the top of the stairs.

"Oh, god. Mary? Mary, is that you?"

That voice. She knew the voice. Of course! "Justin? Is that you?"

"Yes, Mary," Justin cried as Mary hurried down the steps. "Oh god, Mary. Help me! Please, help me."

She stood at the bottom of the stairs, unable to move her legs. The entire basement sprawled before her, its horrors clearly visible. Mary Miller screamed like never before. "Jesus fucking Christ, Justin! Jesus *fucking* Christ!"

In the corner, the antler-impaled corpse of Grandma Miller sagged, an awful expression of fright forever frozen on the old woman's pale, long face, her eyes open wide in horror and surprise. A huge dark stain lay on the concrete below her. Blood.

Against the far wall was the freezer Mary had been so desperate to raid. Its lid was propped open, and a long trail of red painted the front.

Beside the blood-stained appliance lay a blood-soaked sheet with something that looked like a body underneath—a small body.

And in the center of the room, locked in a cage too small for his body to move, was Justin, bloodied and bruised. And he was naked except for a dirty pair of underpants. Around his neck, he wore a studded dog collar. There was a leash attached, and its chain was fastened to the wall behind the cage. "Help me, Mary. Oh, god, help me."

Mary covered her mouth and swallowed her screams. Tears rolled down her cheeks. Finally, her legs moved, and Mary ran to Justin and knelt in front of the cage. "Oh, Justin. I'm sorry! I'm so sorry!"

Justin sobbed and mumbled something inaudibly that sounded like *Junior.*

She patted his head through the bars, then abruptly stopped. Mary noticed something sticking out of the freezer that made her blood run cold. It looked like a human hand. And it was reaching out of the freezer. "Oh, god. No. No. No."

Mary stood and strolled toward the freezer. She knew what... who... she'd find stuck in there before her eyes gave the final confirmation. There, painfully shoved into the twenty-one-cubic-foot freezer, were the naked bodies of Denise and William "Billy" Miller. Portions of their flesh had been carved down to the bone. One of Denise's breasts was missing, and part of Billy's thigh. Both of their buttocks had been slashed, and their heads had been nearly cut clean off their shoulders.

"Oh, Maryyyyyyyyyyy," Justin cried behind her. "It was Junior."

Junior? No. It couldn't be. No...

"You've..."

No. Don't.

"You've been..."

No. Don't you dare say it. Don't you dare.

212

"He's been feeding you Mom and Dad!" Justin broke down and sobbed inside the cage. Mary didn't think he'd ever stop crying again.

Her eyes wandered to the bloody sheet. She tore it away to reveal the dead body of Alex. The child had been stripped, and there were purple and black bruises around her neck—unmistakable handprints. *Junior's* handprints. Mary lowered the sheet and covered up her sister's lifeless body.

The realization hit her all at once. Mary fell to her knees and sobbed. Her parents were not only dead, but she'd been eating them for days. And she had loved how they tasted. Jesus Christ, she would eat them again if Junior waved a plate of their dad's chest or their mom's liver in front of her face. There was still plenty of meat to be had before they spoiled.

Remember, the voice said. And only then did Mary recognize that the voice was her own.

No.

Remember.

No!

Rememberrrrrrrr. NOW.

An Actor Prepares

Two months ago.

In the playhouse in the backyard.

At night.

Huddled inside a sleeping bag with Junior.

They were naked.

And they were fucking.

In the afterglow of their forbidden sex, *Wouldn't it be fun to pretend to be Mom and Dad for a while?*

Her idea. It had been *her* idea. All of it.

Not surprisingly, since she had seduced Junior after school three years earlier. She'd caught him watching her shower through the peephole he'd made in the bathroom and proceeded to give him one hell of a show. When Junior retreated to his room to take care of himself, Mary walked in, dropped her towel, and convinced Junior to fuck her—not that the boy needed a lot of convincing. At that point, he probably would've stuck his cock in a wall socket if she'd told him to.

A month ago.

Mary and Junior skipped their last periods in school. They thought they'd have the house to themselves for at least two hours, but they were wrong. Denise Miller came home early with a headache, only to find Junior and Mary going at it in the middle of the living room. She ran upstairs to call Billy. Mary made Junior finish before they got dressed.

Eighteen days ago.

Justin was out. Alex and Toby spent the night at a sleepover and hadn't come home yet.

Denise and Billy told Mary and Junior they were taking a week off from work and were going to "get to the bottom" of whatever had been going on between the incestuous siblings and put an end to it. If it meant shipping one or both of them off to boarding school on opposite coasts come fall, they'd do it. They'd ask Grandma Miller for a loan if they had to, and she'd almost certainly say yes if it involved sending Junior away. *That boy is no good.*

Mary and Junior left the house, armed with a shopping list and a credit card.

Let's do it, Junior. Today.

Whaddya mean, Mary? 'Do it'?

You know. The game I was telling you about. Let's do it.

I don't think so, Mare. We'll get caught.

No, we won't. They're taking off work.

So? A week. What do we do when the week is up and people start looking for them?

No one will come looking for them. Christ, Junior. We're talking about Mom and Dad.

Yeah, what about Grandma Miller, smartypants? She'll come looking.

And we'll tell her they went away.

They went away. And what then? She's just gonna get her fat ass on a plane back to Vegas?

So, we kill her, too. The bitch is almost a hundred years old anyway. She's lived long enough.

Ninety-five.

Whatever. It's still older than dirt. No one's going to miss another old lady.

I don't know, Mare. This sounds crazy.

It is *crazy. But it'll be fun.*

What are the rules again?

Mary told him the rules and explained the game one more time to Junior.

What happens when it's over, Mary? How do we win?

Well, ideally, 'we' win by making the others break character.

And we can kill them when they break character?

Totally kill them. Those are the rules. We all have to stay in character as soon as the game starts.

But what if you break character, Mare?

She'd laughed. *I won't. You know I'm a wonderful actress. Remember* Fiddler on the Roof? *Hell, even I thought I was Jewish for a while there. I made mom get me a menorah and everything that year.*

It was Junior's turn to laugh. *Oh, I know, Mare. You wanted everyone to call you "Mary Rabinowitz" for seven months.*

Mary Eliza Alice Rabinowitz, Mary had corrected.

You've got them all fooled, haven't you? Especially Grandma Miller. They have no clue who you really are.

But you do, don't you, Junior?

I hope I do. Otherwise, I could be agreeing to just about the dumbest thing I've ever done.

Just think of it, Junior. You can sleep in the same bed as me every night. And you can kiss me. And you can...

Okay, okay. I'm sold. I know the kids will play along, but what about Justin?

Leave Justin to me.

Yeah, he is kind of a puppy dog around you, isn't he? Stares at you with them pathetic little puppy dog eyes, hangs on your every word. I do think that boy is a little slow. He never catches on to anything until it's too late. Can't see a storm coming for miles on a clear day, that brother of ours.

Leave him be. You're just jealous. He's my own personal Fido.

Oh, he'd probably hump your leg if you'd let him.

Or kill someone if I asked him to, she whispered. *Fido will do whatever I tell him to, whenever. Leave big brother to me.*

Alright, Mare. Alright. But don't come crying to me if I have to put him down if he steps outta line or tries to man-up, you hear?

Arf, arf, shed barked at Junior.

So, we're doing this? For real?

We are, Junior.

Damn, Mare. I'm so excited. I've got a boner. Just look at it. Has it ever been this big before?

I know. I can see it. Let's go back and surprise them. Do it now. Get them out of the way. Then we can screw in their bed. We can always go shopping late before the kids come back from their sleepover.

Mare, I think that's the best idea you've ever had.

217

Family First

They circled back to the house and entered through the basement.

Denise was first.

Mary stabbed her in the back several times and then slashed
her throat open in the middle of the kitchen. Billy heard the
commotion from the upstairs shower. Clad in only a towel, he
opened the door to investigate.

Junior sliced Billy's face, cutting his mouth so deep his jaw
nearly fell out. Mary stabbed her father in his legs and then
in his groin. When Billy fell to his knees, Junior slashed at his
throat.

Mary and Junior kissed as their father bled out in the hallway.
Their kissing spilled over into what had been their parents'
bedroom, but was now *their* bedroom. There, still covered in
their parents' blood, Junior fucked Mary so vigorously the bed
frame nearly broke.

Later, they emptied the basement freezer and hid their
parents' bodies inside. The murderous couple scrubbed the
house clean with bleach and threw out any potential evidence in
a bin five miles from their place in a shopping plaza. They went
grocery shopping and stocked up the pantry with everything
they thought they'd need for a week. By early afternoon, the

kids still hadn't come home, and Justin wasn't due back for another few hours, either. They retreated to their new bed and made love one final time before the game began.

Justin came home first. Junior left him alone with Mary. She wore a low-cut tank top and no bra. While she explained their parents had left to take care of something with Grandma Miller, Mary leaned into him and bent down to give him an eagle's eye view of her tits. Mary told him how their parents left Junior in charge and suggested they all play a game to pass the week without incident. Ogling Mary's cleavage as she ran her hands up and down his arms, Justin would have agreed to Mariah Carey's "All I Want for Christmas" being on repeat nonstop for a year if she'd ask. This game sounded far more doable.

The other kids agreed right away, as Mary knew they would. Alex and Toby spoke in unison as they so often did and laughed at things no one else seemed to hear.

Junior, since he was the one "left in charge," assigned the roles.

Toby, I want you to play Alex. And Alex, I want you to play Toby. Remember, you can't use your real names at all. No slips! From now on, you sleep in each other's beds, too, and wear each other's clothes.

Wait, what?

That's right, Alex. You're going to be Toby from now on. And Toby is going to be you.

Justin, you're the family dog. Fido.

But we don't have a—

We do now, and you're it. You're always saying every year at Christmas how you wish we had a dog.

Yeah, I'd like to have a dog. I didn't say I wanted to be one.

That's your part, Justin. No breaking character. From now on, you're a dog, not a person.

Fine. Arf. Arf.

And last but not least, my Mare. You're the shy but dutiful and devoted housewife.

Okay. Got it. I can do that. Do I smoke?

Um, what?

Do I smoke cigarettes? Or drink wine?

No. You're a goody-goody. Very Florence Henderson. But even more modest. You like to call me 'dear.'

Okay. Got it. 'Dear.' This is going to be so much fun.

And you?

What's that, Fido?

Who are you going to be?

The hardworking, loyal, beer-drinking man of the house, of course. So in one hour, the game begins. It starts as soon as I, the hardworking dad, walk through that door and say, 'Honey, I'm home.' Any questions before we start? Once the game begins, you cannot stop to ask questions or break character for any reason.

What happens if we do?

We take your ass to the pound, Fido.

The Postman Always Dies Twice

And now, Mary remembered everything. She'd been so lost in her character that Mary had forgotten her *true* self.

I can still win.

They had to go. Toby. Justin. That was the true aim of the game. They had to die if she and Junior were going to escape together and live happily ever after.

She turned to the cage and held the knife out in front of her. *I'm sorry, Justin,* she thought. *Poor, poor Justin. I really am.*

Justin had his head buried in his arm, crying full force by then, so he didn't see Mary approaching. He never knew just how close he'd come to death that afternoon. Mary was less than a foot away from the cage, knife at the ready, when the front door buzzer went off.

Justin gasped and looked up, the tears suddenly gone.

"Now who the hell can that be?"

Mary raced up the stairs.

"And you, dog, be quiet!"

She hid in the dark and waited to see who their uninvited guest was. Outside the door, Mary heard the excited but strained breath of their visitor. A moment later, the knob turned and in strolled their mailperson, Bob Buchanan.

Fucking Bob.

He closed the door and mumbled something. The old man reeked of vomit, and Mary could smell him from across the room where she hid behind the couch. He whipped out his pitiful phone and waved it around like a flashlight. Then he walked down the hall into the kitchen.

Mary lay in wait, debating what to do. He'd broken in, essentially. She could always say she felt threatened, or she thought he was a prowler. It wouldn't be hard to rustle up a truckload of snot and tears. Mary Miller truly was the greatest actress alive. She'd more than given that Streep woman a run for her money. Either way, no matter what the cover story was, Bob had to go. If he didn't call someone now, like the police, he was bound to later. Or just keep coming back. This fox had poked its nose into her henhouse one time too many, and she knew just how to skin a fox.

Bob walked back through the hallway into the living room, moved to the basement door, and pulled it open. "Hello? Is anyone there? Are you hurt?"

"Helllp meee."

Mary's heart stopped cold. *Fucking Fido. Shut up, stupid dog.*

"All right, I'm coming for you."

Don't do it, old man. Don't fucking do it.

But he did do it, and that's when Mary knew she was going to have to kill the mailman, Bob Buchanan. And she wondered about that nosey bitch next door...

The End of Bob

Justin howled as Mary buried the knife into Bob's chest. "Nooooo!"

Blood spurted up and smacked her in the face. She pushed the knife deeper until the blade was embedded right down to the handle. Mary shook her head as the old man's eyes dimmed to black.

"Maryyyyyy?" And then Bob checked out.

"No more foxes in the henhouse. No more foxes." Mary laughed half to herself.

"Why, Mary? Why?" Justin cried.

"Because he was going to ruin the game. And I have to win."

In the kerfuffle of Bob's murder, neither Justin nor Mary heard Junior enter the house and descend the basement steps. He stood motionless on the middle step and surveyed the fresh carnage, nodding with approval.

"Damn, Mary. You went and killed the mailman," Junior said with a huge smile. "Ah, there she is. There's my girl. I thought I'd lost you. It was like that goddamned Fiddler on the fucking Roof all over again."

"You almost did. I liked being Mrs. Miller, Mr. Miller."

Junior took the remaining steps two by two and threw his arms around Mary. He pulled her into a tight embrace and kissed her mouth passionately. Justin shrieked in horror as Mary wrapped her bloodied arms around Junior and returned the kiss.

"Are you ready to win this, baby?" Mary said, pulling her lips from his at last.

"Oh, fuck yes, Mare." Junior kissed Mary deeper. "Fucckkkk, yesssssss."

"Let's do this. End game."

The pair separated and turned to their brother, still locked inside the cage.

"Have you spayed or neutered your dog?" Mary laughed.

"Not yet," Junior chimed in. "Not yet. But we're about to."

Justin screamed, a sort of half-human, half-dog scream.

"Come to papa, Fido. Come."

The Whole Enchilada

Something was wrong. Most definitely, something was wrong, Joanne Garriga thought as she zeroed in on the front door of the Miller house with her binoculars. Bob had been in the house for too long and he hadn't so much as sent a text. *He did know how to text, right? I asked him that, didn't I? I'm sure I asked him.*

The Miller house just now looked wrong to her. There was no other way to describe it. What had been a nice, normal enough looking house on a tree lined street now looked as though it had been put together by someone who'd never really seen a house before, only read about them in books. It was like everything from the wood, to the nails, to the windows and the roof itself was just off kilter the tiniest bit. A fraction of a fraction of inch, perhaps not even that much.

You might not even notice if you were taking a casual glance, but Joanne Garriga never took a casual glance at a anything in her life. And she knew every inch of the Miller house by heart, the exterior anyway. And it wasn't right. The facade appeared to be melting away at a snail's pace as she stared at it, slipping off like the house was shedding its very skin.

"Oh, Bob. Stupid old Bob," Joanne Garriga mumbled to the house that had swallowed the mailman whole. Oh, he was dead, she was sure. Joanne tisked and set down the binoculars with one hand while pulling the blinds open wide with the other. "Devil may care at this point."

Behind her, Joanne's husband lumbered up the stairs. "You at it again? Jeez, woman, don't you have an off switch?"

"I think we need to call someone, hun."

He stood in the doorway, close enough that she felt the disapproval oozing off his skin. "Who do we need to call about what, Jo?"

Before her very eyes the Miller house shifted again. It was slight, so slight that if you blinked, you'd miss it. But Joanne Garriga would never close her eyes for an instant or turn her back on that house. "I do think something very wicked and very foul this way comes."

"What nonsense are you going on about?"

The Miller house flickered. Flickered. She'd seen it with her own eyes. There, and then not there, and then back again like an apparition. Oh how that though chilled her bones. "The police, hun. Call the police. Do it now. Before it's gone for good."

She didn't know if she meant the house or the story itself, or the whole enchilada, but either way, somehow Joanne Garriga knew all of hell was about to break loose on St. Augustine Place. And she had the only front row seat.

The Winner Takes It All

They put Fido down, which wasn't hard because the broken-down beast had no fight left within it. Truth be told, neither Mary nor Junior enjoyed putting it out of its misery. It was far more satisfying when they put up a fight, kicking and screaming, to stay alive—like good old Cast-Iron Cassie Miller.

Any other bitch would've died instantly, but not Grandma Miller. She hung there, moaning and bleeding out for what seemed like hours. Junior hadn't even stayed until the end. Justin, unfortunately, drew the short straw on that lot. The two pitiful creatures looked at each other from across the room, moaning and groaning, unable to do a goddamned thing to help the other.

Mary and Junior had stabbed Justin over a dozen times apiece. He didn't scream or cry, just lay there, taking it with a smile. During the frenzy, Mary heard something coming from the back of Justin's throat. Not the gurgling of blood one would expect, but something like a melody, a song. It was broken up, but she recognized it easily. Everybody knew "Humpty Dumpty."

And while Mary thought he was delirious, lost in a fevered brain dream, Justin Miller was at a tea party. The finest tea party that ever was. He was dressed to the nines in a coat and tails. The thick mane of auburn hair atop his head was slicked back and shiny. He was sitting at the longest table he'd ever seen. It stretched as far as the eye could see. He sipped tea with his pinky raised, noshed on cinnamon-flavored biscuits, and told jokes and reminisced with Toby and Alex. There were no tears, only laughter and smiles.

Where is this place?

The kids shrugged.

Is this real?

Definitely, Alex said.

Toby nodded in agreement.

This is it, isn't it? The thing that you both do?

Uh-huh, the kids said in unison. They all laughed at this.

But... how? How on earth do you do it?

Alex shrugged. She looked at Toby, who also shrugged.

He appeared pensive and then said, *You just have to think about it real hard, and then it happens. The things you see just happen, but I don't really know how.*

Does it hurt?

No. Toby laughed.

It tickles. Right here. Alex pointed to a spot on the back of her head.

Tickles?

Yeah, Toby agreed. *It feels like a billion little fingers tickling your noggin at once.*

Interesting. Alex, could you pass me one of those double chocolate biscuits?

But of course, big brother. Would you care for more tea?

Yes, please.

They sipped their tea. Alex chomped on a biscuit, and the crumbs rolled down the front of her blouse.

228

I'm sorry I wasn't a better big brother to you both.

Silly. You were the best big brother, Alex said with a beaming smile. She rose from her chair with grace and shuffled around the table to throw her arms around Justin. Then Toby did the same.

Oh, big brother, the kids said almost in one voice.

In the world that wasn't a tea party, Justin Miller's heart beat for the last time. No one spoke over the body or said words of comfort.

Junior uttered, "Stupid dog... ruined my good tank top."

Mary said not a single word for her dead brother.

At the same time, Alex and Toby lowered their heads.

It's done, isn't it?

Yes, Alex replied.

Okay. I'm okay.

She reached across the table, which now didn't seem so wide, and squeezed Justin's hand. And somehow, he knew in that moment of connection what lay ahead. Not just for him, but for Junior and Mary as well. That knowledge made Justin smile.

They're coming for you, Alex said, turning to Toby.

I know.

Are you ready?

Yes.

Off to See the Wizard

"Would you just look at this? Who knew Justin had such good meat on his bones?" Junior laughed as he sliced a chunk of flesh out of his sibling's leg. "What the fuck, Mary? Are you crying?"

Mary turned away. "No. I'm not."

"Bullshit, you are! Look at me."

"I don't want to."

"Look at me, Mary."

She quickly scrubbed the evidence away from her eyes and turned her head toward Junior. "See."

"Nice try there, Mare. I can see, you know."

"I can't help it. Sorry. I was fond of Justin. He was a good boy."

Junior laughed, digging the carving knife deeper into Justin's thigh. "The tastiest cuts are down near the bone. The meat's real tender and juicy. It's what we had last night. Leg o' mom. You seemed to eat it up, if you pardon my French."

"That was Mom? I thought it was Dad."

"Nah, that was Mom. Dad's starting to spoil. I hate to waste the meat, but really, he wasn't as good as Mom, anyway. I don't know why."

"What are we going to do about *him*?" Mary kicked at Bob

Buchanan.

"Damn, Mary. Why'd you have to kill the mailman?"

"You would've done the same thing."

"Yeah." Junior laughed. "But people will come now."

"Eventually."

"Ticktock. Ticktock."

"We have some time."

"To kill." Junior winked at her. "We'd better get the show on the road if we want to be vamoosed by the time some other nosy fuck comes looking for him." Junior shook his head and sucked a wad of air through his teeth—a sound Mary loathed. "Stupid, stupid man."

Junior stood up and wiped his bloody hands on his T-shirt. He threw the knife into the wall, and it slammed into it with a clunk. "Haha! Not bad!"

"Yeah, you should go pro."

"Don't sass me, Mary. You know I don't like it when you sass me."

Mary stepped toward him and grabbed his crotch, making Junior groan. "Looks like you like it quite a bit, Junior." She squeezed harder, then released her grip. "Well, Mr. Miller? Shall we kill our last living child?"

"We shall," Junior wheezed.

"To Oz?" Mary asked, offering Junior her arm.

"To Oz," he replied, linking his arm with hers. "Is that a line from that fucking *Fiddler* show?"

"No, you moron. It's from *The Wizard of Oz.*"

Prayer for the Dying

Toby sat on the edge of Alex's bed, primed and ready. The taste of that yummy tea and biscuits lingered in his mouth. No matter what played out next, he wanted to go back to the tea party with Justin and Alex. He needed Alex's charge to run his battery at full capacity. What he'd done earlier in the day had been a good start, but it only happened because Alex had given him a slight push from the other side. She'd need to give a hell of a lot more than that if Toby was going to surprise Junior.

And Mary.

Toby still couldn't believe what he'd seen when his mind reached out to Justin. Alex had told him to try it. *Insisted.* Junior thought he'd choked all the life out of her, but she'd lived just long enough to see Justin caged before she finally died in the basement. Alex had been far too weak to do anything, like open the lock on the cage. And she sensed Justin knew that, too. Alex tried calling out to Toby, even Justin, but she found herself mute. Her power was running on nothing but fumes. She really didn't even know what she would have done, anyway.

Even with Toby, the most she'd been able to do up to that point was move a few small objects around. Moving physical objects in the real world drained more of their batteries than mind jumping. And she didn't really know how it all worked—how long they needed to rest to recharge their cells, how they even did that, or how any of this was even possible.

Alex considered Toby the stronger of them, but where the power excited her, it scared him. And for good reason. A few days after the joke with their mom's keys, they'd tried moving her whole car, and it triggered an awful asthma attack. By the time Denise raced in with the inhaler, Toby had gone cold, his face a terrifying shade of purple and blue.

Going that deep into his mind had almost killed him. And now, to win the game, he'd have to go even deeper. The puffer was all but empty. To win, Toby would have to die himself.

Do you want to die a victim, like Justin and me, or die fighting? Alex asked from inside his head in their secret place.

Fighting. But...

You're scared?

Yes.

Don't be, silly. I'll be right there with you.

I know.

Help me, Obi-Wan Kenobi. You're my only hope.

Toby laughed.

Death isn't so bad, brother. But don't worry. I'm not going to let you die.

Promise?

Yes. I promise.

Okay... Hey, Alex?

Yes, Toby?

I love you.

I love you, too.

Sore Losers

"Toby, come down here, boy!" Junior called from the bottom of the stairs.

It's time.

Mary draped an arm around him. Behind her back, she held the blood-soaked butcher's knife while Junior concealed a hammer in his back pocket.

"Oh, Junior. This is so exciting."

"Shush, Mare.."

"I'm sooo wet," she whispered in Junior's ear, flicking her tongue at his earlobe.

"Not now, woman. Later," Junior snarled. "Hey, Toby! You up there, boy? Get your ass down here."

Toby hopped off the bed, a surprising spring in his step. Without touching it and using only his mind, the bedroom door flew open with such force it nearly popped right off the hinges. Toby took a deep breath and slipped deeper into his mind until he was in that special place. The back of his head was so itchy, but he resisted the urge to scratch the skin right off and soothe the gray matter beneath. The light hairs on his arms and legs slowly rose to attention. Every hair on his scalp began to dance and sway, like they were under the influence of static electricity. The green color drained from his irises until there was nothing but white, and then slowly, the white pulsed and cracked before shimmering like shards of glass.

Toby made his way down the hall, toward the landing. His skin was fiery to the touch, a reddish glow surrounding him as if he could burst into a ball of flames at any second.

"Toby!" Junior yelled.

He stood at the top of the stairs and looked down at his "parents."

"There you are, boy!"

"Oh, my god," Mary screamed. "What's wrong with your eyes?"

Toby said nothing, only stared at them with his shimmering eyes that also glowed red.

"Toby?" Junior sounded uneasy.

"You lose. Both of you."

"What are you talking about, boy?" Junior asked nervously.

"Your eyes! My god, Junior, what's wrong with his eyes?" Mary shrieked. "I can't look at them."

"You broke character," Toby said. "Both of you."

Junior looked at Mary and laughed nervously. "You believe this shit? The balls on this kid."

"Rule number three—punishment for breaking any of the rules shall be both swift and severe," Toby said, devoid of any emotion.

"You don't get it, kid, do you? The game is over. And we've won, which means you lose."

Mary shrieked again, turning away. "Junior, I can't... those eyes... He's in my head. He's in my motherfucking head, Junior! Get him out!" Mary clawed at her temples. "Out! Out! Out!"

"Shut the fuck up, Mary." Junior removed the hammer from his back pocket and waved it menacingly. "Game over, kid."

Junior took a step forward.

The shimmer in Toby's eyes pulsed, glowing bright, then dimming.

"Swift." Something pulled again behind Toby's eyes. "Punishment is good."

The Miller house shook violently right down to its foundation. It sounded like a thunderstorm had descended on the living room as a series of booms and crackles reverberated through the walls and floors.

Junior fell backward as the house shivered, his body smacking against the wall. Losing her footing as well, Mary wobbled around before landing right on her ass in the middle of the living room floor.

"Junior!"

"Punishment..."

"Now... you die, boy." Junior hurdled the steps, taking three at once. He made it halfway to the top before—

"...is severe."

"No, Junior, don't!"

Junior cocked the hammer over his shoulder. He lunged up the remaining steps, letting out a savage, inhuman howl. As Toby's eyes throbbed and glowed brightly, Junior's body froze like a statue. His eyes, however, darted about wildly.

"Mmmmmggrrrrrrr," Junior groaned.

"Oh, my god, Junior!" Mary hobbled to her feet.

The house rocked again, even more forcefully.

"You're a bad man."

Toby's eyes shone bright red, growing in intensity as though a dimmer switch turned up until their glow was blinding. Whatever had been holding Junior in place released him, and he growled as he took a step forward.

Crack!

Junior screamed in agony as his right leg flew forward, folding over the knee. The leg stayed in that unnatural position for a moment before swinging back lamely, fragments of broken bones protruding through the skin.

Despite the increasing pain, Junior hobbled up another step.

"A very..."

Crackkk.

Junior's other leg.

He dropped to his knees, howling in pain. Determined, he used an arm to lift each of his legs up to hobble-walk up the remaining stairs.

"Very..." Toby wheezed. His lungs began to give out.

Crack!

Junior's left arm broke.

Crack!

And then his right arm jiggled like a plate of gelatin. The hammer slipped from his hand and slid down the stairs.

"Bad..."

Crack!

Junior's spine snapped.

"Man."

There came a final, deafening *crack!* as Junior's head spun a full one-eighty. He gawked at Mary through wide, horrified eyes.

"Mare...," Junior gurgled as blood poured down his chin.

"*Junior!*"

Junior's head fell to the side, and his limp body swayed, guided by the heavy weight atop his shoulders. Blood sprayed over the back of his shirt. His head fell back like a lead weight, crashing into the edge of the top step. A deep, dark river of red

237

flowed out of Junior's agape mouth and rolled down the stairs step by step, making a gruesome red carpet.

Junior's wrecked body slid down the stairs, picking up speed until it crashed into the wall at the bottom and then slithered down the wall slowly, leaving a trail of red ooze. His crumpled body lay at the bottom of the stairs, twisted unnaturally in multiple directions, a grisly pile of flesh and broken bones.

Mary rushed to it.

"No! No! No!" She untangled the mess of broken bones to find his head. Mary caressed Junior's blood-spattered cheek. Tears rolled down her cheeks as she shook his body. "Junior!"

Toby panted. He couldn't find any air. The shimmer in his eyes dimmed.

Alex? I can't breathe.

Toby felt dizzy. His body stumbled back a step before he could steady himself again.

"*You!*" Mary sprang to her feet, the knife shimmering in the dull light. "I'm going to kill you!"

She charged the steps, a wild and insane look on her face, her mouth stretched into a revolting grimace-smile, but before she could even put her foot on a single step, the staircase split down the middle with a piercing boom. Thick splinters of wood flew as though a bomb had gone off. Fragments whizzed past her face, scratching at the skin, and blood oozed from the various cuts. When a heavy splinter landed in her left eye, Mary hollered in pain and her hands shot to the wound. The knife fell to the floor.

Toby collapsed onto his back, and his eyes regained their green tint as he settled back from that special place. Below, he could hear Mary's shrill cries and curses, but knew she couldn't reach him upstairs. Not yet, anyway. A dull ache settled in his chest. There was air all around him, but he couldn't seem to breathe enough of it in. Every breath pierced his lungs.

This was the moment that terrified him from the day he first discovered the special place with Alex. *The cost.* Nothing comes for free. Sooner or later, you have to settle your debts.

He could feel himself slipping away, falling somewhere between here and the special place, but not fully in either. Mary's cries grew more and more distant as the house moved farther and farther away. Numbness overtook his body as everything went limp and cold. Suddenly, there was no more pain, and the last shimmer of light blew out like a candle in a rainstorm.

Go Time

Alex dragged Toby into their special place. He was still unconscious, but death had not yet claimed Toby Miller. There was still time. She hurriedly pried his mouth open and then stood over her brother, filling his lungs with the air she'd taken from him earlier, at the end of the tea party. She didn't know if this would even work, but it was worth a shot.

It was now, or never. All or nothing. Go time.

Win Some, Lose Some

Mary plucked at the splinter, and bloody tears fell from her wounded eye. It felt like a letter opener was sticking out of her eye socket. She could still see, but her vision was fuzzy. Junior's corpse lay at her feet. *No time for this now. Sorry, Junior.* She looked up at the landing on the second floor and spied Toby's prone body. No sound, no movement.

"Hey," she called. "Hey, kiddo." Mary shambled toward the smashed staircase. "Are you okay up there? Do you need your puffer? I bet you do." She picked up the knife. "I'll get it for you. Let me come upstairs, and then we can go. Just the two of us."

Mary poked her head around the banister, looking for a way to climb the stairs. It would be hard. Not impossible, but nearly. *He looks dead. Let's just go. Find the car keys, and just go.*

And then it hit her.

I won. I won the game.

She *had* broken character with Junior by calling Toby by his real-world name, but that was only a technicality now. Everyone else was dead, so—

"Marrrrryyyyyyyyyyyyyy," a ghostly voice called from somewhere behind her. No, *beneath* her.

She spun on her heels, holding the knife at the ready.

"Who's there?"

"Maryyyyyy," another voice called.

"Wh-wh-who is it? Who's there?"

A long, deep sigh billowed up from the bowels of the house. That chilled her more than the sound of her name.

The keys. I have to find the car keys. Wait. Where exactly is the car? One problem at a time. The keys. I think Junior left them in the—

"Drawer," Toby said, finishing the thought aloud for her.

Mary turned and saw her younger brother standing on the landing. In his hand, a set of car keys jangled.

"H-h-how?"

A horrifying howl rang through the house. Mary covered her ears, but still, she could hear it and the sound of footsteps climbing the basement stairs, getting louder. Getting closer.

"Marrryyyyyyyy," one of the voices crooned.

She ran across the room and slammed the basement door shut. "No!" Mary dropped to her knees and wiggled the paper clip parts, still dangling from the lock. A second later, the lock clicked and bolted the door shut. "Ha! I got you! I got you!"

"Marrryyyyyyyy."

The voice was just behind the door. She could almost feel its foul breath on her skin.

The thing on the other side of the door growled a warning and then pawed at the door. Not with human hands, but animal paws with long, sharp nails. Mary heard the wood roll off the door in slivers as the beast scratched at it.

"Oh, dear god. What *is* that?"

Toby smiled. "Here, Fido. Come to Papa."

The beast howled, and a second later, a monstrous paw burst through the door. And then another. The door rattled. The wood ballooned, then cracked. Soon, the entire door split and came off the hinges as the hellhound burst forward with a ferocious howl.

Mary screamed.

The beast snarled, revealing a mouth of fangs. The animal was massive, well over three hundred pounds. Parts of the beast's skin had been torn away. Its ribcage was visible, as were the bones and tendons in one of its monstrous legs. The creature's eyes glowed an unearthly shade of green.

She ran for the front door, but it wouldn't budge. Mary fumbled with the lock and the knob, but the door wouldn't open. And she knew why.

Toby.

"Open the door! Toby, please! Open the door!"

"Marrryyyyyyyyy!"

Mary turned and saw the ghastly shapes of her undead parents, Denise and Billy, crawling up the stairs toward her. They stared at her through their dead, yellow eyes. Flies circled their faces, and the foul stench of their breath filled the air.

"Please, Toby! Stop this! Stop this!"

The beast, Toby's nightmarish vision of Fido, leaped onto the couch and lowered the front of its ghoulish body in a play-bow position, ready to pounce on Mary. The long, mangled hair on the hound's neck rose into horrific hackles.

Denise and Billy reached the top of the stairs and pulled themselves along the floor in a series of frightful movements, brownish puss oozing from their mouths, sliding over their black teeth. Behind them, another form became visible—Grandma Miller, the antlers still protruding from her chest.

"Marrrryyyyyyyyyyyy," Grandma Miller bellowed.

Mary shrieked and covered her ears again, and Fido barked at her.

"Marrryyyy.   You alwayyysss were myyy favoriiite," Grandma Miller said.

Mary's body crumbled to the floor.

Her undead parents inched closer to her as Grandma Miller stepped into the living room. Fido let out an ear-piercing howl that rattled the entire block. Outside, several car alarms sang into the night.

She looked toward the second-floor landing, and the last thing Mary Miller saw was the figure of her brother, Toby, standing beside Alex, hand in hand.

A second later, the undead horde summoned by her siblings tore Mary Miller apart from head to toes.

And that was how the game ended.

The House of Horrors

Taken from social media posts:

@Lynda2269BX: OMG, is it true? They're all dead? And eaten? (emoji)

@AndyL__FL: Fuck, you heard? I don't know. All I know is there were a lot, and I mean a lot of cops and ambulances. And a shit ton of body bags.

@Lynda2269BX: Garriga said something like eight bodies? They found eight bodies or parts of eight bodies in the house? They'd been there for weeks. (emoji) Fucked up, man. *Fucked up*!

@AndyL__FL: Jeez. Imagine the smell? (emoji) There go your property values.

@Lynda2269BX: For real, though. Ain't nobody gonna wanna live next to the horror house.

@JohhnyRocketRide11030: (leaked crime scene photo) *She was fucking ripped apart*! This is some real *American Werewolf*-type shit!

@(anon): They were a weird-ass family. Bad vibes.

@(anon): Mary watched my dog once. Never gave me back his food. (emoji) Dog was weird after.

@(anon): Mary liked to hurt things. Weaker things. I saw it in grade school. No one believed me. She was a damned good actress even then. Had the good girl image down. SMH.

@(anon): PM me if you want to hear real stories about Mary. The girl was wild.

@(anon): Anyone seen crime scene pics yet? Dying to see inside that house!

@(anon): Forget crime scene pics... anyone got pics of Mary... naked? Why are the psychos always hot?

@(anon): Y'all need Jesus.

@JohnnyRocketRide11030: I heard Mary once decapitated her pet hamster and drank it's blood. True?

@(anon): All I know is one day she had a pet rodent, and the next...

@(anon): Her mom walked in on her sucking its eyeballs through its tiny skull. Sick.

@AndyL_FL: Blood lust? Were they vampires? Anyone ever see them during the day?

@Lynda2269BX: Satanists?

@(anon): Seriously... Y'all need Jesus.

@(anon): This is why I use the GoodNeighbor App! Busybodies unite!

The New York City Gazette, Late Edition:

"House of Horrors Found in the Bronx"

Copy by Jonathan Everstein. Photos by Janice Summers.

In what can only be described as a scene lifted straight out of a horror film, police made the shocking discovery of the remains of at least six persons in a home on St. Augustine Place in the Bronx. Some of the bodies were severely decomposed due to extreme heat and others were found in pieces. Police have been unable to identify all the remains, although preliminary evidence suggests the bodies are that of the residents, the Miller family. The body of U.S. Postal Service worker Bob Buchanan, 47, was also discovered in the basement. Police Chief Randall Peters declined to comment on Buchanan's presence, saying only that the investigation is "ongoing."

According to social media posts, the Millers were: Denise, 41; William, 42; Justin, 17; Billy "Junior," 15; Mary, 14; Alex, 12; and Toby, 11. Stay tuned as this tragic story develops.

Clip from Action-7 NEWS:

Reporter: I'm standing just up the road on St. Augustine Place in the Bronx, the scene of a series of brutal crimes. Beside me, is a neighbor and friend of the victims, Joanne Garriga.

Reporter (cont.): How long have you known the Miller family?

J. Garriga: Oh, my gosh, for years. Our kids grew up together. We moved in around the same time.

Reporter: And how would you describe the family?

J. Garriga: Nice? I mean, they were just your typical, all-American family, you know? Denise and Billy worked. The kids went to school. They were good kids. Mary was the sweetest thing. Always said hi. Offered help. I just don't know how something like this can happen here. It's a quiet street. Everybody knows everybody.

Reporter: So, you don't believe the reports that—

J. Garriga: No. Absolutely not. Nobody ate nobody in that house. I bet my life on that. There's just no way. No. But I knew something was wrong. I knew it. I was the one who called the police, you know?

Clip from Live at 6 with Katie and Jarrod:

Jarrod: So, we have a follow-up on that terrible tragedy out of the Bronx.

Katie: It just makes me so upset to think about it.

Jarrod: Yeah, it's a real tragedy. We have Alexander Morris in the field. Are you there, Alex?

Alex: Yeah, Jarrod. I'm standing here in front of the Miller house on St. Augustine Place in the Bronx. It's been six months since the bodies of eight persons were discovered in the house behind me, and police have no conclusive theories about what exactly happened inside this house of horrors. Neighbors want to see the house demolished. One neighbor, a Joanne Garriga, called it a 'stain on the neighborhood.' Others claim it's haunted, and they don't want it to become a place for kids to perform acts of mischief in. Police, so far, say they're unwilling to see the house torn down as the investigation is still ongoing. Chief Peters said his department will not rest or leave any stones unturned, and they will unravel what happened inside the Miller house.

Taken from The New York City Livewire:

Copy by Andrew F. Murray.

It's been one year since the police made the horrifying discovery of eight bodies in the infamous Miller house on St. Augustine Place—including seven members of the Miller family and postal worker Bob Buchanan. As of this writing, the body of Toby Miller, 11, remains missing. Anyone with any information on the whereabouts of Toby Miller should telephone police immediately on (347) 555-2200.

With the case growing cold and no leads or suspects, Chief Peters is expected to tender his resignation in the coming weeks. The house has become a hotbed of tourist activity, attracting morbid curiosity seekers and ghost hunters alike. Police urge visitors to stay away, citing that the Miller house is still an 'active crime scene.' Family friend and neighbor, Joanne Garriga, has put her home up for sale.

"It's just crazy. We can't stand being so close to it, knowing what happened there. And we hear funny things coming from inside the house. Singing. Laughing. Like children's voices. I'm not saying the house is haunted, but..."

No matter how far she went or how many miles Joanne Garriga put between herself and the Miller house, every night, she heard it in her head—the sound of Toby and Alex playing. And every night, as she lay her heavy head on her bamboo neck pillow to sleep, Joanne Garriga was haunted by the gnawing feeling that she should have called someone sooner. That she should have trusted that nagging feeling in her gut from day one that something was wrong.

Better late than never, she'd say to herself, even as she signed copies of her best-selling book, *The Evil Next Door.*

Better late than...

Children laughing. Playing. Teasing and taunting.

In her head.

Joanne Garriga knew it was time for her to move.

Again.

Epilogue

Shall We Play a Game?

It began as most games do.

On a hot summer afternoon.

With a group of bored, suggestible kids gathered in a basement.

Siblings. Two boys and a girl. The girl was the eldest.

Their parents were upstairs.

The game had been the middle boy's idea.

It was something he read about on the internet. Someone played it miles away in America. And it sounded fun, like an extreme version of playing house.

There were only three rules.

One: Once you have been given your role, never break character. Ever.

Two: The house is home base and a safe zone. Anywhere inside of the house is fair game, and anything outside the house is out-of-bounds. The basement, however, is the only forbidden zone and is strictly off-limits for all players.

Three: Punishment for breaking any of the rules shall be both swift and severe.

Once the game begins, there is no turning back. No one can

give up. It must be played through until the end.

He went around the circle. "Do you want to play?"

"Yes."

"Yes."

He asked, "You know what this means, right?"

"Yes."

"Yes."

He asked, "And you're absolutely sure you want to play?"

"Yes."

"Yes."

He took a sheet of paper and tore it into thirds. On each piece, he wrote a separate role.

Wife–Mother. Religious. Vegetarian. Wine drinker.

Husband–father. Hotheaded. Smoker. Lazy.

Child. Female. Aged 13.

He folded the pieces of paper into small packets and then placed them inside a baseball cap.

One by one, each selected their role.

He asked again, "You're absolutely sure you want to play?"

"Yes."

"Yes."

He pulled a revolver out of his knapsack and pointed it upstairs. "Then let's play."

The kids went for the stairs.

She stopped him.

"Hey, what's this game called, anyway?"

He smiled. "Staycation."

Acknowledgements

To: YOU
Fr: ME
Subject: Don't give up.

I had nearly given up. Thrown in the towel. Put away my quill and ink for good, as it were. *Nearly.*

I was having a healthy debate with myself about this very topic when something in my inbox caught my eye so dramatically that I almost drove off the road to read it. (*In case you're wondering, I was stopped at a red light when I perused my inbox.*)

The email was from Andre and Natasha at M4L Publishing, wondering if my horror novel *Staycation*, this very book, was still available. Meaning, if I hadn't sold it to another publisher, could they publish it?

The Universe sent me a sign in the nick of time.

Fast forward to now, standing on the precipice of a long-held childhood dream coming true, and I find I am so enormously grateful to so many people who had a hand in making this dream become a reality over the course of many years of my days on this globe.

I must give thanks first to Andre and Natasha, and everyone at M4L Publishing. Thank you for believing in me, *Staycation*, and for reaching out just one more time to check in. You changed everything.

Special thanks to Melissa Prideaux at M4L for tightening my words.

I would never have set words on a page if I hadn't been blessed with amazing teachers who nurtured, supported, and encouraged me. Patricia Lobosco, your friendship is a gift. William "Harry" Rettino, our adventures will always find their way into my novels. Hank Adams, someday I hope to live up to all the ideals you saw in me.

To my most significant other, partner in crime, world explorer, and couch buddy... Dana DeFrancesco, thank you for always seeing the best of me, and for giving me the space to be me.

Family often unintentionally provides the best material, and mine is no exception. I thank you Dad for the love of reading, and I wish you were here to see me published. And to my sister, Noelle, it's just me and you, kid.

Friends are the family we choose, and I would be lost without mine: Irin Israel, for everything; Melissa Nelson, for being my biggest fangirl; Loralee Callaghan Janus, for making me try to be the person you see; Rosie Finizio, for seeing me when it felt like no one else did; Juliet Bowler, fate brought us together, and we chose to stay that way; Danielle Hanily, my other sister, and fellow adventurer; Elisabeth Colabraro, my favorite non-reader; Tony Willert, for being there when the world was new to me, and helping me discover who I was; Donna Ingargiola, I Vant to Bite Your Finger and for that first kiss in your closet.

Extra thanks go to the best copy editors in the biz, Two Red Pens; fellow Jersey Shore resident Rogena Mitchell-Jones, and, from Down Under, Colleen Snibson. Friends who became family.

And finally, thanks to my awesome beta-readers, for your

wisdom, insights, and encouragement: Melissa O'Neal, Donna Cuccio, Bethany Elkin. THANK YOU! I keep you guessing, but you keep me writing.

Writing is essentially one person, sitting alone for hours, days, months, sometimes years, putting one word at a time down on the page until it blossoms into a novel, but the truth of it is that it really takes a village. A village of love, support, kindness, empathy, and patience. Thank you to my village, whether I've named you or not. *This belongs to you.*

The most valuable lesson I have learned about the process of writing, although not always been able to practice, is to be your own biggest fan. Don't just be a member of your fan club, be its president. Permission granted to order personalized swag.

And no matter what, no matter how dark the day gets, how hard the rain falls, or how loud the voices get, just keep going. Keep on writing, one word at a time. Don't you dare give up.

RJ Clark
March 2023
Asbury Park, NJ

GET EXCLUSIVE BONUS STORIES

Thank you for reading Staycation. While M4L Publishing works across a variety of genres, horror is our first true love. For your enjoyment, below are links for two free horror novellas, on the house.

Simply follow the link and let us know where to send your book. This will add you to our mailing list, but we'll only reach out to let you know about upcoming releases and any future promotions on our existing titles.

Happy reading!

Erased by Andre Gonzalez (psychological horror)
  https://BookHip.com/WJWANDA

Meet Jeremy Heston.

Before he changed history, he was nothing but a young boy with a simple life, never showing a sign of the horror that would one day come.

When tragedy strikes the Heston family, Jeremy's parents have no choice but to admit Jeremy into intensive psychiatric care. Will the therapy help? Or will it give birth to the monster that will lie dormant within for the following 20 years?

Also included: the first chapter of the first full-length Jeremy Heston novel, INSANITY.

* * *

A Poisoned Mind by Andre Gonzalez (sci-fi/alien horror)
    https://BookHip.com/DAWVDFA

The Exalls know no limits.

Jonathon Browne knows the voice in his head.

It belongs to his deadly enemy, but he never expected the voice to take him over, both mentally and physically.

This supernatural force hijacks his body and visits his top-secret government office with a thirst for blood.

With a helpless battle within, Jonathon must get control and escape from his own team before they execute him.

Will a life in exile be his only choice? Or will the Exalls once again claim another victim?

Enjoy this book?

We hope you enjoyed this release from M4L Publishing.

Reviews are the most helpful tools in getting new readers for any books. We don't have the financial backing of a New York publishing house and can't afford to blast our books on billboards or bus stops.

(Not yet!)

That said, your honest review can go a long way in helping us reach new readers. If you've enjoyed this book, we'd be forever grateful if you could spend a couple minutes leaving it a review (it can be as short as you like) on the site where you purchased the book.

Thank you so much!

About the Author

RJ CLARK began his professional career as a child actor and model, following in his famous uncle's footsteps, Stanley Clements. RJ's face was seen nationwide in the U.S. Army "Stay in School" print ad campaign. He also appeared regularly on daytime television, and worked on numerous film and commercial projects before inevitably returning to his first true love, writing.

As a screenwriter, RJ's screenplays won first prize or placed in the top 5 of nearly every major national—and international—competition worth mentioning. His novella, Two for One launched the indie literary magazine "The Instaga-torzine," broken into two parts across the magazine's first two issues.

A native New Yorker, RJ attended NYU, holds a BFA and an MFA. He has lived in all five boroughs, but now calls historic Asbury Park, NJ home with his wife and dog, an Aussillon named Venus.

While RJ no longer works in the theatre as an actor, he provides accessibility services for deaf patrons at live perfor-mances throughout the country. He is passionate about theatre being for all, and enjoys being able to introduce new shows to deaf or hard of hearing patrons.

When not writing, you're most likely to find RJ either playing guitar along the Jersey Shore, taking photographs of cool dogs and musicians around Asbury Park, voraciously reading new books, working on new music, or traveling the world.

A few of RJ's most favorite things include black coffee, chocolate, Stephen King, peanut butter, Pringle's, Truman Capote, tabletop games, the Universal Studios Monsters, horror movies, and David Tennant.

STAYCATION is RJ's debut novel.

Other Titles from M4L Publishing

Horror:

Staycation *RJ Clark*

Salvation *Andre Gonzalez* and *Audrey Brice*

Nightfall *Andre Gonzalez* and *Audrey Brice*

Resurrection *Andre Gonzalez* and *Audrey Brice*

Replicate *Andre Gonzalez*

The Burden *Andre Gonzalez*

Insanity *Andre Gonzalez*

Erased *Andre Gonzalez*

Followed Away *Andre Gonzalez*

Followed East *Andre Gonzalez*

Followed Home *Andre Gonzalez*

A Poisoned Mind *Andre Gonzalez*

Snowball: A Christmas Horror Story *Andre Gonzalez*

Time Travel:

Time Roller *Andre Gonzalez*

Dirty Money *Andre Gonzalez*

Secrets in the Vault *Andre Gonzalez*

Angel Assassin *Andre Gonzalez*

Time of Fate *Andre Gonzalez*

Zero Hour *Andre Gonzalez*

Keeper of Time *Andre Gonzalez*

Bad Faith *Andre Gonzalez*
Warm Souls *Andre Gonzalez*
Wealth of Time *Andre Gonzalez*
Road Runners *Andre Gonzalez*
Revolution *Andre Gonzalez*

Stoner Comedy:
Blue Dream *OG Haze*

Children's:
Lying Monster *Natasha Gonzalez*